SALT

SALT

HANNAH MOSKOWITZ

CHRONICLE BOOKS
SAN FRANCISCO

Copyright © 2018 by Hannah Moskowitz.

All rights reserved. No part of this book may be reproduced in any form without written permission from the publisher.

Library of Congress Cataloging-in-Publication Data available.

ISBN 978-1-4521-3151-1

Manufactured in China.

Design by Amelia Mack.
Typeset in Wolpe Pegasus.

10 9 8 7 6 5 4 3 2 1

Chronicle Books LLC
680 Second Street
San Francisco, California 94107

Chronicle Books—we see things differently.
Become part of our community at www.chroniclebooks.com.

To the bottom of the sea.

MORDE D'EAU

"You were supposed to be on watch."

I open my eyes and settle on Beleza's leather boots stomping to the bow. My neck stings from where she woke me up by stabbing me with her fingernails. She takes Mom's spyglass out of her pocket, unrolls it, looks through.

I get up quickly. "What did I miss?"

"Radar's been going off for God knows how long." She lowers the spyglass. "I don't see anything."

"Let me look."

"Yeah, *now* you're interested," she says, but she hands it up to me.

I know it's around five a.m. without checking my watch, just by the quality of the light, which is barely enough for me to make out peaks in the water. We're floating around the Mediterranean, like usual, pointed vaguely toward the Iberian Sea. Or at least we were when I drifted off.

"There might be something due west." I hold the spyglass where it is and tuck her head underneath my hand to guide her to it. "See?"

"Mm. What's our speed?"

"Six knots. Seven. Between six and seven."

She raises an eyebrow at me. "That before or after you fell asleep?"

"Give it a rest, I was out for a second."

"Indi."

"It's supposed to be Oscar's watch anyway."

"*Indi.*" She points. "See that?"

"Shit."

"You're gonna want to increase that speed about now."

"Oscar!" I yell.

Our brother scrambles up from the cabin. "I'm awake!"

"Something's coming," Beleza says. "Where's Zulu?" She's already made it to the headsail, and she's gripping it hard, winding the line through her fingers for traction, getting ready to tack against the wind. When it comes to hunts, I know what my siblings' six hands are doing as clearly as I do my own.

"Which side?" There's Zulu, running up from the cabin behind Oscar. Her voice is like a little bell.

"Starboard," I say. "Get the harpoon gun."

"Got it! What is it!"

"We don't know yet."

"I hope it's a fuegodor!" she says. Our last hunt was a fuegodor. Zulu always wants it to be the same monster as last time. If we somehow took down a monster the size of Africa who spewed poison goo and shot bombs from its eyes and ate ships in one bite, she'd be hoping our next hunt was another one of those.

"We're not in Spain, *stupid*," says Oscar. "It's not going to be a fuegodor."

"*You're* not in Spain, stupid," Zulu mumbles.

Beleza hushes them with one hand—a skill she learned from our mother—and straightens her quiver with the other. "Oscar, did you sharpen the knives yet?"

"Just mine and Indi's. Mine's here. His is"—he pauses and digs around the ankle of his boot—"here." He holds it out to me.

"You think it's gonna get up on deck?" I say to her, quietly enough that the kids won't hear.

"I'm just being prepared." Beleza picks up her bow from where she's stashed it at the helm; she was doing some target practice earlier, taking out a few innocent fish with her poison arrows. Normally she keeps it in the storage locker, but not normally enough that it isn't warped all to hell from the humidity and the spray.

She hasn't finished sliding in her arrow before there's a roar that, if I weren't in our family, I'd describe as *otherworldly*. But it isn't. It's this world, this sea, and it's closer than it was a minute ago.

Shit.

It goes on so long, this gurgling, vibrating growl, louder than our air horn, louder than Monaco on Bastille Day, louder than fuegodors, no question. Louder than anything I've ever heard besides—

"Morde d'eau," Oscar says.

Beleza nods and swallows. "Get the blowtorch. It's gonna come up."

"And the big hooks, right?"

"Uh-huh."

This is going to be our first big hunt without our parents, and if that ever had to happen, I wish it were against a monster I really knew. Morde d'eaus are rare, vicious, and terrifying. They're nine-tentacled (nine? It might be ten. Beleza would kill me if she knew I'm forgetting details like this), three-meter-toothed monsters whose only weaknesses are fire and, thankfully, Beleza's poison arrows. But all those do is paralyze—and not for very long, not in a thing the size of a morde d'eau. It's going to take a quiverful to even pause it.

"Get her harness on," I tell Oscar, and he helps Zulu without argument. It's different when a hunt's starting. We're not the kids who were just bickering at each other; we're not brothers and sisters or orphans or people. We're weapons.

Zulu gets attached to the mast—she's small, and we don't need her getting swept out to sea—but the rest of us stay untethered because we might need to make some quick moves, and because the fact that we're going without harnesses makes us feel like we're strong enough to go without harnesses. Even if that isn't true.

Oscar gives Zulu's leather strap one last tug with his teeth. "All right, you bastard," he says, at the ocean. At the monster. "Let's do this."

It's four, maybe five seconds of silence, and there's the roar. It vibrates under our ship, and then up rises the head and thick neck and two suctioned tentacles, each slimy cup bigger than my face. I was hoping it wasn't fully grown. Looks like I'm out of luck.

Our boat quakes.

"NOW!" Beleza yells, and Zulu fires up the blowtorch and waves it around, shrieking, to distract the monster. It rears back and hisses like it's supposed to, leaving Beleza to take an arrow out, lick it—like always—load it, and shoot it straight into the roof of the morde d'eau's mouth.

The monster spits it out like a toothpick.

I grab one of the hooks and say, "Oz, come on!" and we heave it over the side and toward the morde d'eau, trying to both wound it and drag it closer so Beleza can have a better shot. They have skin like armor, though, and our hook bounces off and almost pulls Oscar off the edge from the weight of it. I grab him by the waist and Beleza screams something at me while she readies another arrow, but I can't hear it, can't hear anything over the roaring and its breath whipping our sails around and God, we do not have the right boat for this, this thing could swallow us whole—

"ZULU, TORCH!" I yell, and she hands it over and I grab Beleza's bow and ignite the end of her next arrow.

"Eyes?" Beleza asks.

I ready another arrow. "Eyes."

Two flaming arrows take out two monster eyes. It opens its mouth to scream, and this time Oscar's ready with the hook. I run over to grab some of the weight and he swings it up and into the thing's mouth just as it lurches onto the deck and we hear our boat start to crumble.

"Shit. *Shit*," I say.

Beleza either doesn't notice or doesn't care that our boat's getting damaged. "Burn it, Zoo!" she orders, and Zulu's there in a second with the torch, burning through its skin, detaching the head, filling the air with the smell of burning blood and monster.

It's over. Oscar's bleeding. We're all gasping.

We are us again. We're still orphans. Our boat is still a piece of shit.

We're still some of the best damn sea monster hunters around.

I still hate it.

Beleza wipes sweat off her forehead. "Let's haul it up," she says. "Zulu, go start some water."

SING-ALONG

Butchering is Zulu's job. She stands up on her stool with our good knife, the one we have to make sure to keep as dry as anything in the cabin can be, and saws with that in one hand and thwacks with a machete in the other. *Hack hack hack.* She cuts off massive steaks and spears them onto chopsticks we saved from the Dragon Inn, the Chinese food place back in Nerja we went to last time we were in Spain. We already promised Zoo we'd stop there again next time we're that far east, but for the past day and a half we've been headed toward Sicily to meet with someone we only know from Mom and Dad's journal.

Beleza's idea.

Zulu keeps cutting and Oscar starts the burners while I make Beleza open her mouth. "Spit," I tell her, and hold a cup under her mouth.

She spits. "You worry too much."

"Those arrows can paralyze a damn monster, you gotta stop licking them."

"It's good luck."

"I'll remind you of that when your teeth fall out."

She crosses her eyes at me. "So what were you dreaming about, little brother?"

"Mermaids," I mumble. Might as well just tell her, she'll tease me until I do.

"You know they're not real," she says.

"Shut up."

"You know they have *tails*," she says.

"Still have boobs!" Oscar volunteers.

Beleza glances behind me. "Oscar, watch Zulu with that knife."

"She's fine," he says, without looking at her.

I finish wiping down the inside of Beleza's mouth and open my first-aid kit. This is my job. Zulu does most of the weaponry; Oscar, despite how surly he is with us nowadays, charms locals and tourists alike and keeps food in our stomachs; and I stitch up cuts. Beleza used to be first mate, but that changed a few months ago. Now I'm first mate to her captain, and I think a part of her thinks I'm going to try to wrestle control away from her or something, because every time she has to get me to reach something she can't or haul in a hook that's too heavy, it's with the same narrowed, *don't get any ideas* kind of eyes.

I tug on the bottom of Oscar's pants. "Let me see that leg."

He shifts weight off it. "It's fine."

Beleza says, "Oscar, listen to your brother."

She's examining her mouth in the rusted mirror above our rusted bathroom sink. It's not much of a bathroom. It's barely big enough to turn around inside. This ship has no real appliances, not even a real oven or stove, and our solar shower on the deck leaks and only holds a gallon of water—which we have to get through our reverse-osmosis machine, so that's a whole process—at a time. The result of this is that we're sweaty and dirt-blotched and we pee with the door open. This whole boat is pretty much a piece of crap, but our good boat, our real home, disappeared along with our parents, and all we could afford with the money they left was this third-rate fifteen-meter wooden schooner that's probably been around longer than the beastie we just took down. And he's got to have been in his eighties, judging by the tooth decay. We've seen morde d'eaus before, but that was when we were better armed and a hell of a lot more prepared—and it looks like no one's going to mention this is the first thing we've taken down by ourselves. This wasn't supposed to be a hunting expedition; we weren't even planning to stop in France, and we sure as hell weren't planning on shooting down any French monsters.

I peel the cuff of Oscar's pants away from his sticky ankle. A ton of blood. "You got yourself with the hook again," I say. That's a lot easier to do than it sounds. The hooks for monsters this big are a meter and a half wide and *heavy*. Oscar's big for his age, like me, but his age is twelve, and it takes a lot of force to haul those things off the deck. He needs to stop leaning into them.

"Whatever, I got the thing."

"Sit down. I gotta stitch this."

He plops down on the ground and pouts. "Great."

I light a match to sterilize my needle and tie off a piece of dental floss. "You okay up there, Zulu?"

"Yup!" *Thwack*—off goes a tentacle.

I give Oscar's ankle a squeeze before I slide the needle into the bottom of the cut. He groans and thumps his head back against the floor in time with Zulu's chops. "Stop that," I say.

"Ughhhhhh."

"Seriously, cut it out." I put my hand between his skull and the floor and give his head a rough squeeze the next time he throws it down. "I'm not treating you for a concussion too. You'll just have to die in your sleep."

"Jerk."

"Mm-hmm." I hum a stupid song I made up when he was a baby and wouldn't sleep—the lyrics are *Oscar, you smelly bastard, go the hell to sleep*—to distract him until I'm finished stitching. "All right, buddy. All done."

He flexes his toes, slowly. "Thanks."

"Yep. I'm starving, start roasting those."

Oscar picks up a skewered piece of meat, and for no damn good reason, yanks on one of Zulu's pigtails. Just like that, she's crying.

"Why do you have to antagonize her?" Beleza says. She slams the bathroom door behind her—we only close it for effect—and comes out and scoops up Zoo.

"I didn't do anything!" Oscar says.

"Bullshit, we all saw it."

"She was in the way."

"Get your damn story straight."

Oscar kicks the heavy pots hard enough that they rattle but doesn't say anything.

"Careful with that leg," I say. "That's my handiwork."

Zulu sniffles into Beleza's shoulder.

Once the meat's done, everyone mellows out. French monsters don't have the best texture, but the flavor's always good. Just like French people, my dad used to say.

We don't have a proper booth down here for eating, and unless we're docked, sitting down for a decent meal is kind of a useless venture anyway, since three-quarters of your attention has to go to making sure your plate doesn't slide away. So we sit around the Bunsen burner and eat our steaks right off the chopsticks while we lean against the bunk beds, my back against one with Oscar rested against my shoulder and Beleza sprawled out in front of the other. She's tired. Zulu, on the other hand, is full of energy now that she's cried and eaten, two of her favorite pastimes, so she's singing and skipping around the Bunsen burner, making everything shake. The sea is gentle, rocking us like babies.

"*Yo, ho! Yo, ho! A pirate's life for me!*"

"Zoo," Beleza warns.

"*Drink up, me hearties, yo, HO!*"

"Zulu," Beleza says, more sternly this time. "What have we told you about pirates?"

Zulu stops singing but not skipping. "It's just a *song*."

"Tell me what we've told you about pirates."

"They're useless scum not even . . . shouldn't be allowed to be *people*."

"That's right."

"So can I sing PLEASE?"

On a bad day, Beleza would get up in a huff, stomp up to the deck, and not come down for hours. I'd find her straddling the wheel and staring out at nothing, or pacing and adjusting the sails for changes in the wind no one can feel but her. Or maybe she'd even snap and yell at Zulu; we don't do it much, but we're not perfect. We're two teenagers and two kids on a tiny boat in monster-infested waters. No one's a hero, here.

But it's not a bad day. We killed a monster. And that's all it takes, in Beleza's world, for it to be a good day. No wonder the monster venom never makes her sick. My big sister *is* monster venom.

And so today she tips her head back, her hat slipping off a little, and says, "Yeah, what the hell. Devils and black sheep, right?"

/

It only takes about two hours before it's very clear that our rickety *Salgada* isn't going to make it to Sicily in its current condition. We've sprung a leak on the starboard side, where the beastie bit into it, and our hasty patch job isn't going to hold forever, and the same magnetism that lets us detect monsters in our radar sometimes shorts out our ham radio, and even after half an hour of fiddling with it I can't get a hint of a signal.

"Our spare sail is rotting," Oscar says.

"We're out of crackers," Zulu contributes.

Beleza sighs.

"Marseille?" I say.

"I guess." She pulls out her compass. "Brush me up on my conjugations. I hate French."

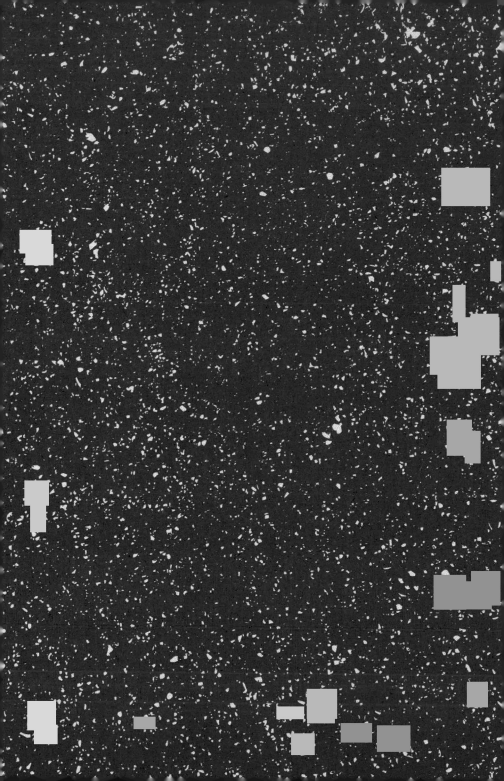

THE NIGHTMARE

I should have expected that talking about a risky ship right before I went to sleep would have me waking up gasping a few hours later, but I didn't.

I'm burning hot, like I always am after a nightmare, leaving sweat on my sheets that's going to soak in and get cold by the time I go back to sleep. If I go back to sleep. We don't have any spare sheets. We'll do laundry in Marseille, maybe. Pick up some more canned food, maybe see if I can find a bookstore so I'll have something to read for our next stretch of flat sea. This is how I keep myself focused after these hunts. I think about boring things. I think about things we'll do the next time we reach land. Laundry, spackling, stocking up on supplies, getting the radio fixed, maybe finding a girl. It's going to be a busy trip. If I come up with enough things we have to do while we're there, it means we'll make it there in the first place.

We'll make it.

Above me, Beleza's snoring in her bunk. Zulu is curled up by my feet; she sneaks into my bed a lot in the middle of the night. I slip out carefully and I'm cold right away, my T-shirt already settling into a cold damp mass hanging off my shoulders, so heavy it's making me feel like I can't breathe. The Mediterranean is warm, but not at night, not in a ship cabin. Not out of bed.

I dig around under the bed for my flashlight. It rolls out of my fingers a few times, tossing with the boat, before I finally grab it. Both my sisters are heavy sleepers, and Oscar is up on deck for watch tonight, but I still shield the light with my hand as best I can while I rummage through Beleza's stuff. Beleza's been insisting she have custody of the journal lately. She says I don't take good enough care of it, and Mom and Dad are going to want it back once we find them. Like me, she doesn't actually believe Mom and Dad are alive, she's just trying to keep up a brave face in front of the kids, and it's not like we have a lot of opportunities to talk about anything without the kids around. Our ship's the size of a postage stamp. You can't breathe without getting air that's just come out of someone else's mouth. So this isn't an invasion of privacy, we don't have that. Secrets were for Mom and Dad and for landlubbers. Daydreaming about running the hell away from all of this is just for me, but it's hardly a secret.

I find the leather journal and open it carefully. The pages have been soaked so many times that they don't feel like paper anymore, and the whole book is fragile as hell (and

I *am* being careful). In a lot of places, Mom's handwriting is too washed-out to read. Most of the writing is hers. Most of the pictures are Dad's. Were.

We lost them months ago now. It's hard to know how long ago exactly. It feels like three months. Beleza's changed: colder, harder, more ruthless, licking more arrows than she used to. Oscar hasn't been acting any different, but I'm not dumb enough to think that means something inside him isn't broken that wasn't before. Zulu's okay. She cries sometimes, but she's young, and Mom and Dad are always gone—she's six, she has no sense of time. Beleza and I don't agree on how to handle them, I guess, because Bela's always telling them not to give up hope and it's going to be okay, and I . . . well. Someone has to be okay already. Someone has to stitch us up.

The last thing we know is that they were probably somewhere around Turkey. They didn't know the name of what they were after, but that doesn't mean there aren't notes about it in here, newspaper clippings, guesswork sketches. It's a hideous thing, body as wide as its head, eyes like dirty rocks, mouth in a permanent, toothy smile. Who knows if that's what it actually looked like. It's how it looks in my dreams.

They knew it was a big hunt. That's why they left us with a few essentials: the journal, some money, each other. Sometimes they'd take just Beleza with them, or more often just Beleza and me, but not this time. We fooled ourselves into thinking it was just because Oscar's in this rebellious stage where you can't trust him to watch a pot of hot water, let alone a little sister. We told ourselves they'd gone after way more vicious things in the past, that Dad's estimation of its size must have been a joke, that there's no way there's something out there two hundred meters long and almost as wide. But then they just didn't come back. Bela and I know what that means.

Beleza doesn't want to talk about it.

I do.

She just wants to make sure their monster's been killed.

I don't.

This is our big source of conflict lately.

I shiver and try to tug the blanket off my bed, but it's trapped under Zulu. It's okay. I'm fine. I thumb through the crackly pages until I get to the end of the journal, to my favorite part. The part about the treasure.

Ever since I can remember, Mom and Dad had promised us a treasure when we came of age. It was our big reward for being such good shipmates, sidekicks, soldiers. Sometimes they'd tell us that they weren't going after a monster this time—they were going to check on our treasure, to "make sure nobody else has found it." They always came back all smiles: It's still there, it's even better than we remembered, when you grow up it's all yours. We'd beg and beg and tug at their arms and they'd never tell us anything else.

When I was a kid I used to think maybe it was a nice monster. That was my theory. Some sweet little domesticated dragon thing, and we'd live happily ever after.

Now I just hope it's money, like one of those pirate treasure chests. Enough to get Beleza a house somewhere, to enroll the kids in a good school. And to get me the hell away.

Which reminds me, that kid we can't trust to watch a pot of water is in charge of looking after all our livelihoods right now. I head up.

He's sitting with his feet on the helm, watching the sail while he blindly sharpens a knife. "Hey," he says. He sounds hoarse.

I feel his head for fever—you've got to be careful with cuts like that—but he's fine. He leans into my hand a little. He's unexpected, this kid.

I pull over a crate and sit down next to him. "Couldn't sleep?" he says.

"Could. Now I can't."

We're quiet for a while, then he says, "Why don't you talk anymore?"

"I talked last."

"So?"

"So that's how conversations work, Oz. It was your turn."

"You and your rules."

"Don't act like anything about me surprises you."

He smiles and blows dust off his knife. "Guess not." We watch the waves until morning.

VIEUX-PORT

Beleza's in a good mood when we're nearing Marseille, which means she decides we can indulge Oscar's and Zulu's social little hearts and dock in Vieux-Port instead of in Marseille-Fos, where we usually end up when we stop in Marseille. Vieux-Port's always crawling with people; when I was a kid it was one of our favorite places. We were stationed there for a couple months when I was about six, and in December shops open up, selling all sorts of Christmas trinkets. I couldn't get enough. Beleza and I and tiny baby Oscar put miniature Nativity scenes around our motel room with no idea what they even were. Our parents never saw them; they weren't with us for most of those months, because they were investigating and tracking and then killing a diver-munching fantombre nested in Cosquer Cave. Why lubs—the landlubbers who help haul our boat in, walk around with their feet on the ground—think it's a good idea to slap on diving gear and go explore a cave with a reputation for swallowing people up is beyond me, but so are most things that normal people do, because that's what happens when you're a sic from birth, I guess.

That's what we are, *sicarios*—it's Spanish, because as far as most of the lore can tell us the first great monster-poachers were. We're nicknamed sics so we can talk about ourselves in front of the lubs or the garden-variety sailors without them thinking we're there to murder their families or take care of their onshore pest problems (my parents once hunted down a crocodile in Mauritania, but that was for a friend). We don't know how many of us there are, since throwing yourself into the nests of monsters increases your odds of getting eaten by them. Mom and Dad's journal has a list of about forty names of sics they trusted. A good third are crossed out because they lost either that trust or their lives. So essentially, our options for help are limited, which is frustrating because Beleza's nineteen, I'm sixteen, Oscar's twelve, and Zoo's six; we have a moldy, falling-apart sailboat; and my sister has designs on a monster bigger than any of us has ever seen.

Zulu's off the boat in a second, running down the pier, and I give Oscar a look until he grumbles his way after her. Bela finishes hauling in the rope and turns to me and says, "What's your game plan?"

"Find some food, see if I can track down an inn."

"We have money?"

We made some spare cash patching up roofs when we were in Cosenza two weeks ago. Since then we haven't left the boat, so it's not as if we've had a lot of chances to spend it. "We're all right for a couple days."

"I want to get us out of here by Tuesday," she says. I'm about to respond, probably just to tell her it's okay, not to try to talk her into giving us a week to recover—that hunt last night left us all a little battered. But I never know what I'm going to say to Beleza anymore until it's halfway out of my mouth. Then someone comes up to her to talk about money for docking and she works her way into French to argue. With each other, we speak a bastardized combination of Portuguese and Arabic and Greek with a hefty dash of Italian and French when we're discussing food and sailing and a heap of Spanish largely just when we're talking monsters, because Beleza's the only one of us who ever had any hope of learning a consistent language, because Beleza's the only one of us who ever had a home.

The guy talking to Bela is trying to rip her off and she is having none of it. When she's giving me or one of the little ones her trademark spitfire I want to throw her overboard half the time, but when it's directed at some stranger . . . well.

"I'm going to track down the kids," I say to her, and she nods without looking at me and keeps arguing.

It's always strange, trying to get back into the habit of being on land. My legs are wobbly at first, prepared for an unsteadiness that isn't there, but what's always hardest to get used to is how many *people* there are. The *Salgada* is a small ship and it feels like the four of us—and on the rare occasions we would take it out with Mom and Dad while our big ship was being prepared, the *six* of us—are stepping all over each other all the time, but that's nothing compared to Marseille. The guidebook we have on it—we have a lot of guidebooks—says it's the second-largest city in France after Paris, but I've never been to Paris and probably won't ever go. I've never been anywhere not on a coast.

A woman walking in the opposite direction bumps shoulders with me and I almost come out of my skin. It's the invasion of personal space, but it's also the irrational fear I always have that anyone who comes too close to me is going to *know,* like awareness of sea monsters is something you can catch from someone like a cold.

It's for their own good, my mom used to tell me when I'd wake up crying. *If everyone knew about monsters, there'd be a whole stupid lot of lubs charging into the ocean with spears, thinking they could save the world.*

Saving the world is our job.

Zulu and Oscar are up by La Canebière, the main road. I knew I would find them. Every time we dock we all scatter out, but we've never really lost each other, even though we have no reliable way of making sure it never happens. I know how to use a pay phone, *barely,* and I know the thing that girl is fiddling with in front of Café Michele is a cell phone, and that's about it. We're all aliens, really, whenever we're on land. I don't know how to drive a car or read fluently in anything other than Arabic, and anyway from a legal standpoint Beleza is the only one of the four of us who exists. We guess our birthdays, because our parents couldn't remember exactly when they were and most of the time we don't know what date it is anyway. I assume my full name is India, but that's only because of Oscar and Zulu, and I'm never going to know for sure. But there's no reason I'd ever need a full name, anyway. I don't talk to anyone besides my family.

It is what it is.

Zulu's chowing down on shrimp. That girl really can eat. When she sees me she grins and slithers up my legs and into my arms like she hasn't seen me in a week.

I smack a kiss on her cheek. "I hope you paid for that."

"Oscar said he did."

Oscar is very conspicuously not looking at me. Great.

"You have money," I say to him.

"Yeah, and now I *still* have money."

"You're a shit."

He smiles at me. "I never get caught."

"That's not what I'm worried about," I say, shifting Zulu onto my back. "Come on, you two. I'm hungry too."

"I can get you something," Oscar says.

"Yeah, well, how about I get us a pub and a motel?"

"Can't we just sleep on the boat?" Oscar says.

Zulu kicks her feet. "Noooo!"

Oscar says, "You sound like a *baby*, Zoo," and flicks her on the back of her head.

"Stop hitting your damn sister or maybe I'll make you sleep on the boat by yourself."

"Good."

"It's a dry bed for a night. You should be happy."

He shakes himself a little. "I don't like *rooms*." Oscar is a real sic at heart. Always will be. He's got salt for blood.

Right now he's limping a little, and I feel bad. "How's your leg?" I say.

"It's fine. Doesn't hurt."

"Uh-huh. You're walking that way for fun?"

"Yeah, Zulu thinks it's funny."

"I do," she says.

I check the docks to see if Beleza's still by the *Salgada*, but she's not around. She probably left a note up on the deck under the wheel, where we usually do, but I'm not concerned enough to climb up and look. She'll show up. What I want right now is a sandwich and anywhere I can take off my soaking-wet shoes and put down this six-year-old who's getting heavier by the second. For a moment I selfishly wish that Oscar's leg was better just so I could saddle him with our little sister. What a great doctor I am.

There's a boat next to us now that wasn't there before. It's a black thing that makes the *Salgada* look like one of those cruise ships. A girl who couldn't be much older than me is tying it up by herself.

"Do you need help?" I say in French. She doesn't look up.

"Maybe she doesn't speak French," Zulu says.

Oscar says, "We're in France, stupid."

"*We're* in France and *you* don't speak French," she says.

"I speak more French than you do."

Zulu calls him an asshole, in French, and swings her foot out to kick him in the shoulder, which makes me smile, I'll admit. Still, I rub Oscar's shoulder a little, and when I glance back up the girl is watching me.

"Need help?" I try again.

She shakes her head a little and says, "English?" in English, which is just about the only word I know in English. I shake my head. "Arabic?" she tries next, in French.

"Yes!"

"Oh, awesome. Yeah, some help would be great. My piece-of-shit crew left to get drunk already."

I set Zulu on the ground and go over to her. "No way you have a crew on this thing."

She smiles with half her mouth. "You don't know."

"Where are you from?"

"Everywhere," she says.

"Before that?"

"Tunisia. You?"

"I love Tunisia."

"Eh."

"We're from everywhere too." I tie the rope up. "Before that, Portugal." More or less. It was a small island off the coast of Portugal, and I never lived there, although Bela did. I was born on a dinghy about a hundred miles from Algeria.

"I hate Portugal."

"You lying about that one too?"

Now she smiles with her whole mouth. "No," she says. "That one's true. I goddamn hate Portugal."

"What brings you here?"

"Supply run." She looks over my shoulder. "That your boat?"

"If you can call it that. Yeah."

"It's nice."

"You really are a liar."

"And you really are just full of social skills, aren't you?" She slings her bag over her shoulder. It's open and silk scarves and jars of spices are spilling out of it. She's like something from three hundred years ago.

"What's your name? See, social skill."

She smiles a little. "Hura."

"Hi."

"You?"

"Indi. This is Oscar and Zulu."

She takes a minute, then says, "Ahh, I get it. NATO."

"Yeah." India, Oscar, Zulu—they're all words in the phonetic alphabet. If Beleza had been born after my parents got into the business, she probably would have been Juliet, but back then the ocean was just something they dipped their feet in after a long day. I imagine. That's how I like to imagine them back then, peaceful and innocent, so tied to calling their only child Beleza—it's *beauty* in Portuguese—that she's never wanted to grow out of the nickname. Half the time I can't even remember what her real name is.

"Hura," I say, just trying it.

"It's Arabic."

"I know."

"Right." She hoists her bag farther up her shoulder. "I'll see you around?"

"Yeah." I turn and watch her go. Oscar's snickering. "Shut up," I say.

"How was she?"

"What?"

"You're screwing her with your eyes."

"I said shut up, kid."

"Is she pregnant yet?"

"Zulu, kick him for me."

THE INN

Beleza's not at the first inn we check, but she must have described us well because the guy behind the desk, all mustache and overalls, hands us a note from her that says she's trying a place over on Belsunce because this place is a shithole. Her words, but yeah, she's not wrong.

The first place I see on Belsunce couldn't be it, but it looks air-conditioned and I've got two sweaty kids hanging all over my sweaty self, so I step inside just for a minute and there's Beleza on a couch in the lobby drinking a soda.

"You need a shower before you sit on that thing," I say to her.

She takes Zulu from me. "I know, everyone who walks by is giving me dirty looks. It's pretty great. Hey, ZooZoo."

"We can't afford this place," I say.

"Sure we can," she says, with that look that tells me this is the end of the discussion, which either means she knows she has no leg to stand on and she's ending the conversation before I can prove it, or she's already found work for us to do before we leave. I don't know which I'd even prefer.

Beleza passes out room keys and we get in the elevator and continue to get dirty looks from lubbers who don't like smelly sics, apparently. They're all in sunglasses and bikinis, laughing to each other in French with their heads tipped back so far I can't believe their dumb straw hats don't fall off. I don't know if they're laughing at me—they're talking quietly and quickly, and my French isn't good enough to keep up—but I'm sure they are, I'm just *sure*, and I'm getting that throat-squeezing anxiety that I hate, the one that throbs this mocking melody into my head: *You'll never be normal, you'll never be normal, you'll never be normal.*

Beleza takes Zulu in for a shower with her and Oz flops onto one of the double beds and tries to figure out the TV. "Let's order room service," he says.

"Room what?"

He holds up a booklet from the nightstand. "They had it in that place in Anafi, remember?"

"I remember you robbing the kitchens."

Oscar flips through the booklet. "That was *my* service to *their* rooms."

"You got us kicked out." I lie next to him and nudge my shoulder against his. "That was you."

"Nuh-uh."

"It was. All your fault."

"I'm seriously hungry though."

"I know, me too."

"So what was with that girl?"

"You were with me the whole time. You know exactly as much as I do about 'what's with that girl.'"

"She's hot."

"Too old for you."

"Too young for you."

Zulu and Beleza come out of the shower, naked and squeezing their hair into their hands. I gather Zulu up and get her into pajamas and work on her hair some. She got Beleza's and Dad's looks: olive skin and curly hair that takes an hour to comb the seawater out of. When Zulu was younger she'd scream when we tried to brush her hair, but she's sweeter now and stares openmouthed at cartoons while I work out knot after knot. It helps that Oz is being nice to her for once, holding her hand and sometimes walking his fingers over her knee, even though he's probably only doing it to get out of having to shower.

Beleza feeds the little ones granola bars while I'm in the shower and comes into the bathroom while I'm opening all the bottles around the sink. "What the hell are you doing?" she says.

"Look." I swipe my finger on her hand. "They're all lotion."

"What?"

"These bottles. It's like five kinds of lotion."

"Steal them all."

"Oh, trust me."

She smiles. Moments like this hurt now, because there she is, there's my real sister, the one who used to be my partner in stupid crime, who used to daydream with me about a life out of the business, who taught me how to read. There she is—and then she blinks and she's gone again.

"We have to go," she says. "After we put them to bed."

"Go where?"

"Got the signal from one of the guys behind the desk when I checked in. I used the Belasco ID." We have about fifteen different fake IDs. There's a complicated system about when to use each one, depending on whether we want other sics to be able to find us. Last name Belasco means we're looking for information, and we drop it into conversation whenever we can, waiting to see if someone picks up on it. Three or four times we've run into other self-identified Belascos and gotten to help them out. It was kind of awesome.

But I didn't know we were looking for information here.

"He slipped me the address for a pub," she says. "Maybe they know something."

"About Mom and Dad?"

She shrugs, shuts me out, because that's so much easier than addressing the odds that any old sic is going to be able to help us. But then she adds, "Whatever they know. It's always good to have work."

"You think someone's gonna pay us to chop the heads off some beasties?"

"Hey, we gotta pay for this place somehow."

"I hate you, you know that?"

She kisses my cheek. "I do, yeah."

We go back into the room and pull back the sheets on the bed farthest from the door. We hug the kids—even

Oscar—and tuck them in. Zulu cuddles up against Oscar, and he groans but doesn't shove her off, at least not right away.

"There's a knife in the safe," Beleza whispers to Oscar. "Combination three-three-five-two." We always keep weapons nearby, as if sea monsters are going to rise out and knock on our door disguised as a maid. But whatever. I was once in a battle with a monster who spit a baby monster out of its throat mid-fight who flew through the air and bit me on my ankle—point being, stranger things have happened.

"It always feels like the first time," Beleza says to me, in the elevator.

"Leaving them?"

She shakes her head. "Being on land."

"You think?"

"All dusty and shit," she says. "We don't belong here."

"Salt in our blood."

"Exactly."

She's distracting me from making her answer my actual concern. "So seriously, your theory is this guy can help us find the thing that got Mom and Dad?"

"I want a cigarette."

And yep. That's about as close we get to a conversation about them. "Yeah," I say, "me too."

We stop at a place that looks likely and shell out even more of our money to buy some. "I don't know anything about this guy," Beleza says in Greek, because she must think the saleslady looks both suspicious and definitively non-Greek. "I haven't even talked to him."

"So he doesn't know we're coming."

"Lubs have phones, I don't know. The guy at our hotel might have told him." She blows smoke through her nose. "And a sic onshore might as well be a lub. *Retired*," she says, like it's the ugliest word she knows, and Beleza knows the word for pulling a monster's brain out through its nose. "We headed the right way or what?"

I read the directions again. "Addresses are so confusing."

"Right?"

"I always get tripped up on left and right."

"You should have seen me in Nerja where they measured stuff in feet."

"I did see you," I say. "I live in your pocket."

"Mm, yeah. What's that like?"

"Cold."

"Yeah, that's the sea air."

I lean my head against her shoulder, just for a second. "I know."

The pub is run-down but not seedy, with mismatched glasses and paintings hung everywhere and a dozen tiny chandeliers lighting up the damp-looking wood walls. It's mostly empty—just a bartender, three loud and very drunk teenagers at a booth in the corner, and a guy sitting at the bar in a sweatshirt with his hood up.

"Must be him," I say.

"Mm-hmm." Beleza slides up next to him, all fluid and slow with a cat smile on, and says, "Hi, we're looking for someone." Disturbingly, she learned this from our mother. Although Mom's French was better.

He looks her indelicately up and down. "Really. Who might that be?" He has an accent too, like French isn't his first language, but I can't place what it might be.

"I don't have his name," she says. "Just know he's expecting me. I'm Francesca Belasco."

"Belasco?" the bartender says.

Beleza and I both look up. The bartender studies us while he twists a rag inside a beer glass.

"I thought Belasco was older," he says.

"I'm older than I look," she says, even though she isn't.

Maybe that's why he laughs. "He with you?" he says.

She points to me. "This one is." Now that she knows he's not a sic, she's lost all interest in wet sweatshirt over here.

"All right." The bartender whistles for one of the waiters to take his place and then nods to us. "Come with me."

He leads us back to a door marked *Personnel Autorisé Seulement.* Down that hallway is another office, where he shuts us in and lights a cigarette. He takes a seat in a faded floral armchair behind the desk, leaving Beleza and me to cram onto an upholstered bench on the other side. His office is full of pictures of his family, except for one photo behind his head that any layperson would think was just him holding a very large fish. It's not, though; that's a khenzeer-ma, a deceptively small and very vicious Egyptian monster that can swim as fast as a jet plane. He's right, in that picture, to look as proud as he does.

"I'm Edmund," he says.

"Indi," I say. "This is Beleza."

"Youngest sics I've seen in quite some time."

"We're not officially . . . ," I start, but I don't know how to continue. It's hard to explain that I don't know if we're committed just to this revenge mission or to picking up our parents' business altogether, and that I don't know how set in stone that *we* has to be, that I don't know if I've ever really been a sic to begin with when all I've ever been is a lonely kid on a boat wondering how fast jet planes go. It's hard enough to explain when I'm *not* stumbling my way through a language that isn't my best.

And it isn't until after I've decided that it would be too much trouble to explain, and that it isn't a conversation I'd like to force Beleza to listen to anyway, for me to even consider that Edmund probably just plain doesn't care about my backstory. Why would he? I know he's hunted a khenzeer-ma and he understands sic code. That's all I need to know about him. I don't need to know the names of his children in these pictures.

This is what happens when you grow up in someone's pocket. When you live in a bubble with only the people who know everything about you whether or not you tell them, you have no idea how to act with people who might not care. My siblings and I, we're the most self-absorbed bastards most people ever meet. But how would we know any other way to be?

"We've only recently started taking our own hunts," Beleza says. She's much better at talking to people than I am. Sometimes I think her two years as an infant in the real world made all the difference.

"Well, good timing for me, then. There's a nest near La Joliette—"

"We're here for information," I say. "Not work."

He leans back in his chair, hands behind his head. "I don't know anything."

"Nothing," Beleza says flatly.

He shrugs. "I'm out. I've got the bar now. I got sick of living on crackers and boiled water."

She nods toward his picture. "Khenzeer-mas make pretty good meals."

"I got sick, I wanted a doctor, I wanted a bed. I took out my fair share of monsters. Every once in a while I go out and cut the head off another one."

Well shouldn't he get a damn medal.

"Anyway, La Joliette. Some tourists are complaining that their boats are getting gnawed through," he says.

"Could be a billion things," I say.

"And a guy who works here had a cat onboard his vacation ship who got sucked out. Biiiig trail of blood."

That narrows it down. If you're in France and something's eating cats, that's a "sanglant-dents," I finish.

Edmund raises his cigarette to me. "Huh. Maybe you two are all right."

"If we knock out the nest we need something in return," Beleza says.

"I was going to pay you, that's not enough?"

That *is* enough for Beleza—I can tell by the way she's looking at me—but no, I'm not going to get us into the habit of being hunters-for-hire. That's an excellent way to get us on the road to taking another job, and another job, and another job, all without any real endpoint. And that's not what I want. That's not how I want Oscar and Zulu to grow up. And it's not how I want to be grown.

"We need information on a monster attack around three months ago, somewhere near Turkey," I say. "A large ship went down. At least one."

"Probably," Beleza says. "We don't know for sure—"

"Did you look online?" Edmund says.

I don't know that word. "What?"

"Internet."

"Oh. Yes. Our little brother did." Oscar picks stuff up easily every time we're onshore. He probably got "room service" as soon as we left, the little shit. "They said it was . . . Beleza?"

"An earthquake," she says. "Underground. At least a dozen casualties on an island nearby. Didn't mention a ship."

Edmund studies us for a few seconds, then says, "You said three months ago?"

"About, yeah."

"That's big game you're hunting there, kids."

Beleza leans forward. "You know what it was?"

"No, but I know a guy who might." He takes out a piece of paper and starts writing. "He runs a whole fleet of sics over in Ukraine."

"That's out of our usual boundaries," I say.

He laughs. "That's probably why he's not in charge of you."

"Nobody's in charge of us," Beleza says. Edmund finishes writing, but when she moves to take it he snatches it out of her reach.

"Nuh-uh-uh," he says.

Beleza sighs. "We can take out the sanglant-dents tomorrow night."

"There's a good girl. I'll show you the coordinates for it."

"Indi, take care of this?" she says. "I need a drink."

"Yeah." I watch her go, then I turn to Edmund. "You don't want to talk to her like that. All right?"

He snorts. "You going to hit me, little boy?"

"She will."

"Save it for the beasties." He takes something out from under his desk and unfolds it and waves me over. "Come on, come look at a map." Oh, it's a computer. I've never seen one that small.

I listen to his directions to the La Joliette nest and look at the map and draw pictures and make notes in the back of Mom and Dad's journal. By the time I get out of his office, I'm dizzy from the stench of his sweat and cigarettes and ready to go, but Beleza has three empty shot glasses in front of her and a fourth in her hand, and she's drinking them on the stool next to the guy in the sweatshirt.

She catches my eye. "You cool?"

"Yeah, I'm good."

She pushes her tongue into her cheek to point at the guy next to her. "I'm gonna get out of here, then."

"Okay."

"Yep. See you in a few." Sweatshirt pays their tab and she stands up and hoists her hair over her shoulders. You have to burn off steam somehow in this line of work.

I sit down at the bar to get a drink before I head back, and as sweatshirt guy steps out of the way I see someone at the bar who wasn't here before. She has a purple scarf wound around her neck and halfway up her head and a frosted mug in front of her.

It's Hura.

I leave my spot at the bar and take a seat two down from her. "Hi."

She looks at me, quirks a smile, turns on her stool so she's facing me. "Hi." I can tell she'd known I was there.

"Any chance you want to get out of here?" I don't have much to lose. Really, in my whole life, I have three things to lose, and they're all already in bed.

She picks up her mug and drains it fast. "Come on." Her eyes are dark and melted, and her smile keeps her lips closed.

I have a feeling I'd follow her anywhere.

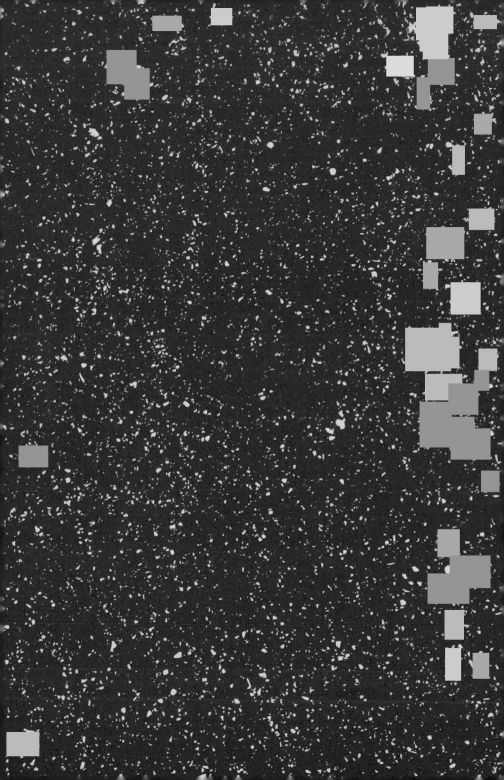

HURA'S SHIP

Beleza might have brought her person to our ship, so we head to Hura's just to be safe. It's even worse onboard than it looked from the dock. I don't know where she came from, but it couldn't have been far. I wouldn't let my brother and sister play with a ship this rickety in a bathtub.

The cabin is tiny and dark and we are efficient. We lie there afterward on a moldy-smelling mattress nailed to a moldy-smelling wall. I feel quiet, different from my usual quiet, because with my siblings there's nothing left to say and yet pressure to teach them and reassure them and respond to them. Here, here I could say anything so there's no need to. There are infinite gaps between us, things she knows that I don't and that I know and she doesn't and absolutely no reason to try to bridge them. Bliss. I almost wish I didn't know her name, just for effect.

She sits up and stretches a little, and I wait until she's done to pull her back down and kiss her.

"I always meet people at that bar," she says. I want to talk to her just because she's speaking Arabic and the familiarity of the words is as much of a relief as the sex was.

"You spend a lot of time here?"

"Mm, more than anywhere else nearby. My heart's in Africa."

"But not Tunisia, you said."

"Not the coast, anyway." She stretches out and exhales with a noise like a growl. "I like the desert. I like climbing trees."

When I was a kid I'd climb masts all day long. I'd hide in the crow's nest and listen to my parents scream my name because they couldn't find me and I'd feel brave and awful and so free.

"So why aren't you there now?" I say.

"Work."

"So what do you do, run a cruise line?"

"Hilarious."

"You're not a commercial fisherman in this piece of shit."

"Hey, be nice to her. Yours has seen better days too."

"If she has, we weren't there for them."

"Yeah, I haven't had this thing for long either."

I scratch the black wood with my fingernail. It gives way like sand. "So not a family heirloom, then."

"Ha. Family." She stands up and walks over to the opposite corner, where there's a bucket of water on the floor. She scoops out handfuls and drips them over herself. The only light down here is from a gas lantern, but it's enough. Her skin is dark and it glitters.

"So what about you?" she says. "You traveling for the money?"

"It's only travel if you're going to and from. We don't have a home."

She shakes out her hair. "Or everywhere is your home."

It's not the first time someone's tried this line on me. It's how Mom and Dad explained it to us when we would ask why we didn't have a house, or a school, or friends. *The whole ocean is your home.* Beleza ate it right up. I like to think I never did, but the truth is, enough of me still gets pulled into the romanticism of it that I think maybe, a long time ago, I believed it too. Maybe I did really want this life, once. Or maybe I have to convince myself I did to make it somehow bearable that it's still all I have.

"How long are you here?" I say, as she crawls back onto the mattress.

"Not sure. Got to try to scrounge up a new boat before I can go anywhere. I'm lucky this thing hasn't sunk while we're on it."

"Ha, I thought about that."

"I hope you can swim."

"What? Of course I can swim."

"I can't swim worth shit," she says.

"Seriously?"

"Seriously. I climb trees, remember?"

"Climb trees, sail ships . . ."

"That's where the money is. I'd do a lot for the money." She shrugs when I look at her. "Most people would. At least I'm honest about it."

"What do you need money for anyway?"

"For buying a new boat!"

"Which you wouldn't need if you weren't trying to make money . . ."

"For my palace," she says.

"Oh really." I stretch my arms behind my head. It's been a long time since I had anyone to banter with who wasn't related to me. Maybe forever.

"Yes. I'm in the process of constructing a castle in Liberia made out of solid gold. Marble staircases. Diamond doorknobs."

"And construction's stalled?"

She nods. "I need to bring at least ten thousand pounds of gold back if we're going to finish the kitchen before winter."

"This boat couldn't support ten thousand pounds of gold."

She kisses my collarbone. "No. Couldn't hardly."

"We need a new boat too."

"I guess your money needs are pretty obvious," she says. "Those little kids."

"Yeah. There are four of us. That's *four* gold castles."

"*Forty* thousand pounds of gold."

"Exactly."

She smiles. "Well, good luck to you."

"You too." I pick myself up. I've done this about a dozen times, met a girl in some port city, had some decent sex or some decent conversation or sometimes both, but I'm still not good at getting myself out. I'm standing there looking for an excuse and I don't have one, and she gets up too, and she's looking at me, all naked and calm, and then there's a yell outside, some heavy bootsteps, the spitting sound of fish hitting the docks. It's morning.

"Go on, get," she says, with a smile and a little shove, and it's impressive, honestly, how solidly and how quickly and how casually this girl just got me to leave. I don't know what her job is and I still think she's a damn professional.

I give polite waves to some fishermen and head back to my hotel room. Beleza's already there, sleeping in the chair with her arms full of Zulu, who must have had a nightmare. Oscar's sprawled out on his stomach on the other bed, his arms and legs like a starfish. I get into the other bed and close my eyes but I don't sleep, just breathe. Beleza's doing her typical snore, and I can hear Zulu sucking on her fingers, and Oscar's silent as always except for the little wheeze through his nose.

The truth is, it's more calming than Arabic. It's more calming than sex.

If I could predict when this feeling would happen, maybe I wouldn't have to stay with them. If I could steel myself—okay, it's Beleza's birthday, it's Zulu's favorite weather, I thought of a joke Oz would love, I am going to feel things now—then maybe it would be okay. I could hold my breath and tell myself I was being weak and codependent for feeling like I needed them, and then it would go away reliably and I would be free and happy and it would all be worth it.

But it doesn't work that way. It's not just when they're sweet, or when they're special, or when they're hurt. It's that I'll come up here expecting just to get some sleep and walk through the door and lie down on the bed and none of them even open their eyes and how much I love them sweeps me away like a tide.

OSCAR

Oscar runs a little bit of a fever in the morning. It's low, but fevers always knock him out pretty good, turn him into the clingy kid he used to be with the bonus adolescent effect of treating Zoo like shit. Beleza has to go work on the *Salgada* and try to bribe some of the dockworkers into helping patch her up with money we don't yet have, so I stay back and take care of him. This is my job. I clean out the cut and take his pulse and get his sweaty bangs out of his face—this kid needs a haircut like I cannot explain—while I squish Zulu into my other side and work on her reading. Emotionally, Zulu is young, but I'm starting to get the feeling she is a really damn smart kid. Her Arabic's already great, so we're working on Portuguese, which I can read about as well as she can, really. Beleza's better, but she doesn't make a lot of time for lessons with the kids anymore. She teaches Oscar points of a sail and Zulu how to care for her machetes and that's about it.

"Why don't camels need to drink?" Zoo says, while we're in the middle of a story about two kids who go apple-picking. I never said she was the most focused.

"They do, just not very often."

"Can they drink saltwater?"

"No, I don't think so."

"Do they eat crackers?"

"Maybe. Write *crackers* for me."

She picks up the pencil with her whole fist. She always holds it so tightly, like she thinks it's going to wriggle away. "In Arabic?"

"Uh-huh."

"There."

She nailed it. "Good girl." I watch her keep writing words—*lantern, chair, brother*—for a while, then say, "You remember Mom giving you crackers?"

"Yeah." She doesn't look up.

"That was good, huh?"

She shrugs.

"You always like crackers now."

"I like crackers because you and Belly give them to me." She licks her finger and rubs it hard over her words, smearing gray across the paper.

"What if Oscar gave you crackers," I say.

"GROSS."

"Shh," I say, but it's too late, because Oscar's stirring a little, rubbing his forehead against his mattress. "Hey, buddy."

He snatches the pillow out from underneath his head and clamps it on top of him. "Shut *up*, Zulu."

She pouts, and I say, "How're you feeling?"

"I'm fine."

"Let me feel." I reach over and palm the back of his neck. He lets me. "Yeah, you're cooler."

He squirms around under the pillow for a minute, then sits up and stretches and gives Zulu a little kick in the back. "Move, shrimp."

"I'm not in *anybody's way at all*."

If I don't get out of this room I'm going to lose my mind. "Oz, how about you take your sister down to the docks to check on the boat?"

"How about *you* take your sister down to the docks to check on the boat?"

"Yes," Zulu says. "How about Indi."

"Because I have twenty euro and you don't," I say. "So unless you think you can charm your way into enough groceries to get us to Ukraine, this is a pretty obvious division of labor."

"Ooh, I'm Indi, I know words."

"*Ukraine?*" Zulu says. She starts digging through my backpack.

"Yeah."

She pulls out my map. "Here?"

"That's right."

"What the hell is in Ukraine?" Oscar says.

"A dumping ground for annoying little brothers."

"Oh *good*," Zulu says.

Oscar pinches her ear, hard, and she shrieks. "Is it a hunt?" he says over her.

"I don't know, and for the love of God leave her alone."

"I'm gonna cut off your hands with my machete," she grouches.

Oscar says, "You don't even know why we're going?"

I pull on my shoes. "It's complicated."

"So Beleza knows and you don't."

"I said it's complicated."

"You really let her boss you around, don't you?"

I finish tying and take the twenty-euro bill out of my pocket. "You can do the shopping job if you shut the hell up."

He grabs it. "Deal."

REPAIRS

Beleza's up in the bosun's chair when I get to the docks, swinging around a little while she fiddles with something, probably something with our radar or the anchor light. The fact that she's up there means a lot of work has already been done; there are two guys patching up holes in the aft of the deck, and there's no way she would have come up to work on the masts if there was a possibility they'd be repairing anything down in the cabin. It's hard enough to explain some details of our boat—all our complicated monster-honed signaling systems, our huge harpoon gun that's pretty impossible to hide—without someone finding our enormous stash of guns and machetes and thinking we're pirates or something.

When I was young, I used to sit in the bosun's chair and Dad would tug on the rope and I'd swing around and around and around and my mom would shriek at him and I'd feel like I was going to fly right off the ship and across the whole ocean. Find some new place no one had ever been and never look back until I landed.

Hura's boat is gone, and I'm pretty embarrassed that I noticed so quickly.

I whistle, and Beleza looks down and grins at me. "Hey! I'm almost done here."

I climb up the ladder and onto the boat. "Need a hoist down?"

"In a minute." She's screwing in a bulb. Anchor light, then. She must have already fixed the radar. She's nothing if not productive. "How's Oscar?"

"Way better."

"Good!"

"Is *Sal* gonna be ready to go out tonight?"

"She better be." Beleza gives the mast a pat. "Somehow we've got to pay these guys."

"Ugh. Great. I gave Oscar the rest of what I have."

"He's probably going to buy a puppy."

"I told him to buy supplies."

"Like I said. He's probably going to buy a puppy."

"I made him bring Zulu."

"Okay, so he's going to trade her for a puppy, then."

"Do you just want a puppy, or what?"

She laughs. "You really think you can make them get along?"

"I don't know. We always did."

"We're not seven years apart," she says, but sometimes she acts like we are. Like she thinks she's been in charge of me her whole life, like it didn't used to be the two of us against the world. Now it's me against everything, or maybe it's her against everything, and maybe that means it's just the two of us against each other.

"Got tonight all mapped out?" I ask.

She nods. "I stopped by and talked to Edmund again. He's charming, isn't he."

"Yeah, he's a catch."

"He says he thinks we're looking at about twenty, thirty. We can handle that no problem."

"Yeah." They're small monsters.

"It'll be good practice for the kids too. Zulu can probably take out one of them on her own. You were what, eight? The first time we went after sanglant-dents?"

"Zulu's six."

"A smart six. She'll be quite the sic someday."

"Mm."

Beleza gives me a look. "Don't start."

"I didn't say anything."

"Being a sic is a good life," she says, and I don't know where she's managed to find any evidence of that.

"There are a lot of good lives," I say.

"This is our job," she says. "It's our duty. Saving the world."

I feel so heavy and tired, like that feverish twelve-year-old is still on top of me. "Do you ever think about our treasure?" I ask.

"What's the strongest current between here and Ukraine, do you remember?"

"Beleza."

"Do you remember."

The journal is in my pocket. I run my thumb over the edges of the pages, pretending I can tell just from feeling which are the pages about the treasure.

Follow the whisper currents.

Thanks, Dad, very helpful.

I pretend that if I check it enough times I'll suddenly know what it means.

"Last time there was a five knot," I say.

"Mm." She looks up at the mast. She's pressing her necklace against her chest. Mom used to wear that necklace all the time, but she gave it to Bela before their last trip. "We should have a spare sail."

"All right."

A HUNT

Oscar shows up with loads of stuff—fruit, cereal, cans of food with pictures on the labels that don't make enough sense for me to sort out what's inside. He dumps it all in the cabin and I say, "How did you get all of this for twenty euro?"

"With my charm and good looks."

"Oscar," I start, and Beleza and Zulu come down from the deck. "We have time for her to get a nap in before we head out?" I ask Beleza.

"Yeah, otherwise she's not going to be much help tonight, are you, Zoo-boo."

"No help at all, help less than a pirate," Zulu says.

I pick her up and put her onto her bunk. "Want a bedtime story?"

"No," she says, and she's asleep within twenty seconds. She has a talent.

While she sleeps, Oscar and Beleza and I take inventory, counting our machetes, our poison arrows, our radioactive bullets. Sanglant-dents are particularly vulnerable to electricity—when I was twelve and we had to take out a load of them we were helped by a very convenient thunderstorm, but the sky is clear tonight—so we finally get to pull out some tasers that we bartered off a questionably moraled policeman in Barcelona just after Mom and Dad disappeared, when Beleza was convinced that the solution for everything was to gather up every kind of weapon we could find, and all I wanted was to believe everything she told me.

Now I say, "They're not going to work."

"Eh," she says.

I pick one up. It's surprisingly heavy. I haven't handled one in a while. Being the ship doctor means the weapons aren't usually my responsibility, and it's kind of an exciting change of pace whenever I can get my hands on them. Tasers are more complicated, too—you have to aim, obviously, and you also have to replace the cartridge between each and every shot, because firing it sends electrodes that fly out and shock the target for as long as you want, which is great when you're taking down a few large monsters, and not so great when you're looking at a school of little ones that aren't really going to need more than a quick zap each.

"Zulu and I are decent shots," she says.

"Also, do we really want to be playing around with electric guns when we're gonna be soaking wet?"

"You only live once."

I look down the barrel. "Mmm. Don't lick this one."

"Bossy little brother."

/

Marseille-Fos Port is where most of the industrial boats are. Last time we came to Marseille, and the time before that, and as far back as I can remember, we parked our ship here. It made more sense; we'd blend in well, so it was easier to get in and out without having to make a lot of conversation and come up with a lot of excuses. It's also speckled on its outer edges with nooks and crannies that are perfect for hiding things, like stashes of illegal weapons or half-eaten monster carcasses. Marseille-Fos Port was often the reason we were coming to France in the first place. Lots of coves and lots of humans to eat means lots of little monsters.

But since we docked the *Salgada* at Vieux-Port this trip, half for Zulu and Oscar and half because our piece-of-crap boat would look more natural in an antique tourist harbor than in one for actual functioning ships, we have a small sail to get to Fos Port before we can start killing beasties. A very, very small sail, small enough that it's unbelievably annoying to have to go through the steps—disembarking and checking wind and counting knots and charging radar and letting Zulu run off one more time to use her last indoor bathroom for a while—when it would be a shorter walk than the one Oscar took to and from the store. I have my harness for mast-climbing and my taser and my small harpoon gun strapped all over me, and it's hard not to be jealous of fat old Edmund, retired in his office with nothing to hold but a dishrag.

I'm at the foremast keeping hold of the headsail while Beleza stands next to me, her eyes glued to her compass, silent but nodding a little every so often to let us know we're still pointed toward the monster nest. When she looks up, I know before she has to say anything to tell Oscar to start to slow down. Part of the reason it's so frustrating that Beleza yells all the time is that she doesn't even really need to *talk* in the first place for me to know what she's thinking.

"Oz, slack," I tell him, and I feel him start to let go of the mainsail. I cast off my sheet all the way and the headsail puffs up and dumps the wind and we slide to a stop to drop anchor.

We're around the site of the harbor, at the mouth of one of the little coves. I can see a few people walking around at the harbor, but they're very, very small, and it's dusk now. I hope they can't see us. Mom and Dad were really good at finding ways to explain themselves when we were caught looking damn suspicious, but we've never had to come up with a lie on our own. Although, as much as I hate to say it, Oscar could probably do a pretty decent job.

"This is the spot?" I say.

"Sort of," Beleza says. "Aft somewhere."

"Behind us?"

"You stopped too damn slow."

"I stopped when—" Not worth it. "Zulu! Look over the stern."

Her little shoes *click-clack* over the deck and I hear her *oof* as she hoists herself onto a crate to see over the railing. She can throw a spear or a Hawaiian sling like a ten-year-old, but she has to work to haul herself upright. That kid's a little joke.

"Nothing!" she says.

"No movement at all?" Beleza says.

"I said *nothing!*"

Oscar says, "Maybe we're in the wrong place."

"We're not in the wrong place!" Beleza snaps. "We've been here for a *minute*, just give it some time."

So we shut up and lean against the railings and the masts and then slide down and sit on the deck, all of us except Beleza, who's a pirate-hatted statue, frozen with her hand over her quiver and her eyes narrowed.

"Bela," I try, eventually. Really eventually.

"Yeah." She's quiet now.

"Maybe they're deep in."

"The cove?"

"Yeah."

"Then they'll come out," she says. "They'll smell us and come out."

"Not if they're not hungry. They've been feasting, he said."

"Should have made Oscar get us a puppy after all," she mumbles. I stand up, and she says, "We can just wait, right? They'll come out." Her voice is desperate now.

"It's getting really dark."

"We're close enough to the shore; it won't get that dark." Begging. She's begging me.

She thinks I'm going to tell her to give up the hunt.

My own damn sister thinks I don't care about saving people.

And isn't that just great. It's not like I even talk to her about wanting to get out of the business. So she infers it from me, fair enough, but then she has to go and ascribe the worst possible motives for wanting to give it up. And she believes it so hard that she's here *pleading* with me about it instead of getting angry, because she's so sure that I'm so set in my desire to let people and cats everywhere get eaten up.

I'm so misunderstood, but the problem is that I am not un-understood.

"I'm gonna swim in," I say.

"What?"

I pull off my shirt. "Into the cove."

"No."

"I'll bait them out, swim right back, you spear them and shoot them. It'll go so much faster than waiting here. And we'll be way more certain we did a decent job of clearing them all out."

Zulu starts to cry.

Beleza tugs me roughly by the skin of my elbow to pull me away from the kids. "You're not doing this."

"One of us has to," I say. "Zulu's obviously not. Oscar's way too reckless."

"Then—"

"I'm the better swimmer and you're the better shot. It makes no sense for you to go down there and leave me in charge up here."

She shakes her head.

"I'll be fine. Get me the snorkel and fins."

She studies me for a long time, then says, "You take more than ten minutes and I'm coming after you."

"Yeah, don't do that."

"Tough shit."

"The kids aren't orphans enough already?"

"Shut up, Indi," she says, but it's all gentle.

The water's cold—around 19 degrees Celsius, which is nice if you're getting splashed, but not as nice if you're plunging in at a moment's notice—and I was prepared for that, though clearly not well enough. Once I dive in I'm treading water and shivering too hard to get the fins on, so they're floating next to me. They look kind of like dead sanglant-dents, which is a little impolite of them.

"You all right?" Beleza shouts.

"Quiet. Yeah." I sink all the way underwater, hating myself for it all along, and hold my breath and stay under until the muscle pain starts to die down. I come up, clear the snorkel, and nod up at the boat. "I'm good."

"Ten minutes," Beleza says.

"Yeah. Sure." I look at Oscar. "Don't let her."

"Okay."

"I can *hear* you," Beleza says.

I slip on the fins, pull the mask on over my face, and clip the snorkel in. "Bye now."

I should have put on the mask before I went underwater. We broke our last one when Oz was goofing around diving off the side of houses on the beach near the Gulf of Izmir half a year ago, so I was trying to be careful with this one. But now my eyes are stinging so badly from the salt that it's hard to open them. Knowing my luck I'll break the damn mask halfway through this without ever really using it for anything but keeping my nose plugged.

No. I have to open my eyes. I'm not going to get eaten by little cat-guzzling monsters because my eyes were bothering me.

The swim to the cove is short, but after that it looks like I'll have to go down deeper than I thought to get inside, and the opening's small—maybe two meters tall by five meters wide. At least I know the odds of any monsters bigger than I am in here are pretty slim. But the top of the opening is about six meters under the surface of the water, and inside, the cove might not even rise up above the water at all. Even monster-free, this could be a death trap.

I take five deep breaths, stretching my lungs, stop mid-inhale so my body's not already primed to push the air out, and dive down. It's dark as all hell. I've got to wonder if this was actually a suicide mission and I didn't know it. Am I suicidal? I've never considered myself suicidal. In our business dying's such an everyday concern that I've never thought of making a big event out of it. It's fitting that that's how our parents went, quietly and undramatically out of our lives.

If I drown right here, that's how I'm going to go too.

That's not good.

I feel around for the opening, my hand slipping over slimy rock. There it is. My lungs are screaming a little already, but I have enough time to get in there and try to swim up for air and still be able to turn around and dart out and up if it turns out there's nothing.

I swim in, kicking hard—hurry up hurry up hurry *up*—banging my feet against the rocks, letting up pressure on my snorkel to the point that it starts to leak into my mouth. Come on come on come on. If there isn't air in here—I give one last hard kick and there, there it is. I break the surface.

I rip out the snorkel and gasp in some breaths, treading water with my legs. I can't feel any silt or seaweed swirling around my feet, so I have every reason to believe the bottom of this cove is very, very deep. When I reach my hand up, I hit the ceiling of the cave before my elbow's even all the way out of the water. This is a tight squeeze, and it's *so* damn cold.

My very unchivalrous and very younger brother thought is *I should have made Beleza do this.*

My very bitter orphan thought is *We should not be doing this.*

So instead I think about blankets and croissants and warming up with a pretty girl, as long as we're doing fantasies, and I blow hard through the snorkel to clear it and I swim. Every tiny fish scares the shit out of me. But sanglant-dents aren't fish. They're stretched-out bodies made of razor-sharp scales and sharper teeth and they have vision that's ten times better than ours in daylight, and in the dark like this, there's no comparison. The fact of the matter is that if they're in here, they've already seen me. And they're not doing anything.

So, that's not terrifying at all.

If they're here, they want me to go deeper. Which means that logically, I should turn the hell around.

But what if they're *not* here, not this close to the entrance, and I *have* to go deeper, but instead I turn the hell around and get out of here and swim up to the ship and tell them I failed and either listen tomorrow to the news that someone's boat or cat or child has been chewed to bits or watch Beleza dive in and not know if she's going to ever come back because she would never turn around, she would keep going deeper, she would not be scared.

And my very younger brother thought is *I want to be like her.*

I keep going.

It's maybe a dozen more increasingly wet breaths through this shitty snorkel when I feel it. Just this slice through the water, so precise and so close to my cheek that the water hits me like a lash.

There's one.

It whistles around my head again, and at the same time, there's a slice on my foot—*shit*, that hurts—and I wince and then open my eyes and there he is, pressed right the hell up against my mask, and God they look a lot bigger when you're not on a boat in the middle of a thunderstorm, and I need to *move*—

I spin around and cut my cheek on a scale and I swim like a kid, splashing and flailing and filling up my snorkel and my mask and this is no way to get anywhere, this is no way to try to keep enough air for the plunge underwater and through the entrance and back into the harbor, and I *know* that, and part of my brain is going excruciatingly slowly enough to really, really fixate on the reality that I have about ninety seconds while my body ignores that in favor of *ow ow ow ow FASTER.*

I'm bleeding now, which is attracting more of them, and I can barely see through the tangle of sharp snicking bodies and then there's a bite right on my shoulder and the thing *doesn't let go*, it stays on me, it bites down harder and harder and harder and—

My hand hits rock. The entrance. I grab as much of a breath as I can and stop on an exhalation because I'm already doing everything wrong as it is and my brain is laughing at me, *laughing*, and these fish sound like laughing and my lungs hurt like laughing and I come up for air as quickly as I can and the thing is *still on my shoulder* but I'm here there's air I'm alive I'm alive but I've barely gotten a mouthful before Beleza yells, "INDI, GET DOWN!" and I don't want to, I don't *want* to, I don't want to go back down ever the hell again, I want a book and a desert and a school for Zoo, I want so many things, I'm so dizzy.

I hear the buzz of the taser and yeah, time to get down.

I stay underwater and swim toward the boat in the straightest line I can. The sanglant-dents aren't as interested in me now that they have a whole boat to gobble up, but the one on my shoulder still hasn't let go and a few more follow me, biting at the backs of my knees. There's a sudden low noise by my head that makes me flinch, and I look and there's a harpoon sticking through one of the sanglant-dents that had been scoping out my neck. Zulu always did have good aim.

I reach the ladder on the side of the boat and start to haul myself up, but I'm so, so tired, and my brother and sisters are a little distracted aiming just about every weapon we own down at the water. I can see Beleza, focused as ever, but she doesn't look at me. She's probably done the calculations in her head and figured out the number of people who would die if she doesn't clear out this infestation versus me.

Which actually makes me feel better, because it's the first moment where I'm sure I'm not going to die. Because she would choose me over anything.

She has to.

I hear laughing, and it's Oscar, laughing like a crazed damn lunatic as he points his taser down at the ocean, frying one after another after another. It's Zulu who eventually reaches down and offers me her hand, and it's far away thanks to her short arms and it's not as if she could really haul me up, but just seeing her there gives me enough willpower to climb the rest of the way. Sanglant-dents I didn't even realize were clinging to my feet and ankles fall off me like raindrops.

"Indi's got one!" Zulu yells as I collapse on my back on the deck, because yep, that thing is still chomped down from my bicep to my collarbone and going deeper and deeper, and this is bad—

"I'm coming!" Beleza calls back, but Oscar's there first, sweat and a smile still all over his face, but he looks at me and he's my little brother and I feel safe, and he says, "All right, Indi, sorry about this," and he points the taser at my shoulder monster and I jerk and go black.

SEAGULLS

One of the things we always catch and laugh and laugh about when we're watching stupid action movies or crime shows in motel rooms is how unrealistic the injuries are. Really, the head injuries. Maybe the strangest thing is how consistent it is from movie to movie—and for kids who live largely without electricity, we have stayed in many motel rooms and seen many, many movies, especially when we were younger and not helpful to bring on hunts—and how much of it revolves around absolute ignorance of how head injuries work.

If this were one of those action movies, I'd be knocked out by the electric shock and the force of my head hitting the deck after my damn little brother tasered me, and I'd get a cut on my head and then spring up with a headache but otherwise be no worse for wear. I'd kick ass with a bandage on my head for a couple minutes, and then after that the bandage would come off and the whole thing would be forgotten, even when I was hit on the head again, and again, and again.

This is not a movie, and I have had a serious concussion, once, when I was ten and playing tag with Oz on the deck after a heavy rain and I slipped and smacked my head against the railing. I was unconscious for about three minutes. I had a seizure. We went to an actual hospital. I don't remember it, because that's how head injuries work, but my parents were very, very scared because being unconscious for any amount of time after an injury is very, very scary.

All of this is to explain how the hunt is now twenty hours and half a country behind us, I was unconscious for thirty seconds *if* that, and I still feel like absolute shit.

Although a lot of that is the bite in my shoulder, or, possibly, the fact that Beleza stitched up the cut in my shoulder. The stitches are so crooked they look like she was trying to write something. Zulu literally could have done a better job—I should have asked her. I don't even know where Oscar was. Everything's fuzzy still, and my voice is hoarse from the electricity, and I'm queasy with painkillers and whiskey and the rocking of the boat from my bunk.

But we hunted the crap out of that shit. After I passed out, they took down every last one of the sanglant-dents I'd baited (I don't know if this was before or after they checked to see if I was okay, and I've decided not to ask), and we docked briefly in Marseille to collect our money from Edmund, who'd already sent a guy out there to swing around with some radar, who said people would be coming up with theories for why there were electrodes washing up on the shore for the next week, but that he wasn't detecting any monster radiation and we did a good job, and here, have this money and have this food and yes, have the name of my buddy in Ukraine who just might have one precious detail about whatever got our parents.

All of this was while I was still very out of it, very useless.

They did fine without me.

Somehow that's simultaneously good news, depressing as hell, and . . . interesting. Just interesting.

I'm cuddling with Zulu in my bunk, feeling woozy and squeezed. We're pushing through the Tyrrhenian Sea now. We're beating, meaning we're sailing against the wind, so we're tacking to get through it, and the zigzagging isn't doing much to help my nausea. Tacking's pretty much the only thing that makes me seasick. Always has been. My mom used to make it some kind of metaphor, about how clearly I was more comfortable going with the flow. Mom's sweet boy.

"Why are we going to Ukraine?" Zulu asks me. She's drawing a picture of a seagull. It's pretty awful. The sooner this girl realizes she's got the brain for a physicist and not a creative, the better we'll all be.

"To talk to a sic."

"What if we run into *pirates*?"

"We won't. Show me your picture." She does. I'm glad she already told me it was a seagull, because I would have no idea. "Very nice."

"Is that where Mommy and Daddy died?"

"Probably not, Zoo."

"But we don't know for sure."

"No, we don't."

"But that's not why we're going."

"Because we think that might have been where they were?"

"Yeah. Or to see if they're alive."

I kiss the top of her head. "No."

"Then how come?"

"This guy knows stuff about monsters that we don't. We're going to get him to tell us stuff and then we'll put it in the journal."

"And then what?"

"And then we'll use it if we ever have to hunt one of them."

"Maybe we shouldn't get the information and then we won't have to hunt any of them."

"That would be nice, right?"

She nods, switches crayons. "What about the treasure?"

"You think about the treasure, huh?"

"Daddy used to talk and talk and talk and talk and talk."

"Yep."

"Do you think there are people there?"

"Where? In our treasure?"

"Yeah."

"Like we find a treasure chest underwater and we open it and all these people spring out?"

"Yeah."

"Probably not."

"Yeah."

PAUSE

So for a few days that's what I do. I lie in the cabin and breathe stale air, and the only bit of the outside world I get is the water that drips down the hatch between the deck and the bunks. My clothes are still damp, because my clothes are always damp, but my siblings are keeping the lamps off down here because I'm still having headaches and with the stagnant air and the darkness I feel more like I'm in a cave than on a boat, and I wake up with nightmares about suffocating in caverns getting tighter and tighter while my brother laughs and bites my ankles.

Beleza's there after one of them. She's only in a T-shirt and a pair of shorts, which looks funny on her. She's usually very intense about her heavy jacket, her holster, her boots, but today it's too hot for even her to try to reclaim the pirate fashion thing, I guess.

She gives me a little smile and pats my knee. "You're okay."

"I am." I sit up, wincing a little. "I am okay." The sea feels calm, I realize. "We're not tacking anymore?"

"Nope, we were jibbing the whole time you were sleeping. Now the wind and us are best buddies."

She shoves me back against my mattress, a little too roughly, and then lies down next to me. "We're not stopping before Ukraine," she says. "Not if we can help it."

I'm too tired to tell her that what would really help is rest. Sure. Monster fight ahoy. "We have enough supplies for that?"

Beleza coughs out a laugh and nods to our kitchenette, where the crate we use as a makeshift pantry is still, almost a week after Oscar's shopping trip, overflowing all over the floor, a few boxes of cookies and plastic containers of applesauce all the way over by the bathroom. "I think we're pretty set."

"That boy sure can make twenty euro stretch, can't he."

She doesn't say anything.

"That's not the kind of haul you can shoplift," I say. "You can't hide fifty pounds of groceries under your shirt."

"So what are you saying."

"I'm saying . . . I'm saying we've got a kid who doesn't know limits and who's used to winning every fight he gets in, who thinks he can play everyone around him like they're chess pieces and who didn't even hesitate before shooting that thing off my shoulder."

"He didn't have a choice."

"He had the choice to *hesitate*."

"So you'd rather he gave you a higher chance of bleeding out?"

"I wasn't gonna bleed out."

"I don't know what you're implying, okay?" She sits up and doesn't look at me. "He's twelve, he's all hormones and anger and aggression, but he's a good kid, okay? I do the best I can with him. What do you want me to say?"

I want you to say *I do the best I can with him, but I can't be his mother,* Beleza.

I want you to say *I can't be his mother because our definition of* mother *is messed up and I will do better than what that word means.*

"I'm implying that he threatened someone," I say. "Held up a store or whatever the hell."

"You really think he's capable of that?" I know she means physically, practically capable, not emotionally capable. Morally capable. We both know he's both of those things.

I say, "Maybe he's not the right kid to be raised at sea."

"Yeah, well, tough shit, you and I are at sea and who else is gonna raise him."

I look at her, and she looks at me, and we have the *I don't have to be on a boat, shut up Indi we're supposed to be saving the world* argument with our eyes so it will be over faster. It still takes so long before I feel like I can look away. I am always the one to look away.

"He's a good sic," Beleza says. "He's going to be a good one."

"He's going to be a pirate," I say, and she stomps up the stairs and out of the cabin so loudly it's hard to believe she doesn't have her boots on.

MATH

"The girls are fishing."

Maybe this sentence wouldn't take me so long to parse if I had some context, or if it hadn't interrupted a dream about choking on someone's hair, but I startle awake and have to lie still, turning these four words in my head over and over.

Oscar's watching me expectantly. He's at the foot of my bed, slouched because he's too tall now to sit up at his full height without hitting his head on the bottom of Beleza's bunk.

I remember when this kid was a *baby*. I don't know if he knows that. He listens to Beleza, even in his ornery twelve-year-old way, and he respects her, and he behaves for her. He knows she's in charge of him. But me, I never know what Oscar I'm going to get minute to minute, so who knows how he feels about me. Half the time I don't even know how I feel about him.

He's carving something. He's really into woodcarving lately.

"Oh," I say. "That's good."

He snorts. "Waste of time. They're not even doing the nets. Just sitting on the deck with poles."

"Just doing it to relax, probably."

He digs his knife into the slab of wood, his tongue squeezed between his front teeth. He and Zulu have the same concentrating face. "All anyone's doing around here is relaxing."

"We're crossing the whole sea. It's a long, boring sail."

"How come we never leave the Mediterranean?"

"We used to, sometimes."

"With Mom and Dad."

"Course."

"They brought us?"

"Those were the trips where they couldn't really leave us behind. They'd be gone too long."

"Where'd we go?"

I roll onto my side. "South Africa. Mexico. Australia, once. Everywhere."

"There are monsters there?"

"There are monsters everywhere."

"How come people don't know?"

"Some of them do. There are sics everywhere too."

"You know what I mean."

"Because there are a billion other things that can kill you," I say. "Tigers, earthquakes, crazy people with guns. Monsters aren't everyone's job."

"So everyone's job is taking out one kind of thing that kills people?"

"I guess."

"So who takes us out, then?"

"Monsters aren't people."

He snorts again. "Ask a monster's mom."

It's not a question, so I don't answer it. "I always wanted to be a mechanic," I say.

"Like for ships?"

"*Not* for ships. Cars or planes."

"They're all the same."

"Like you'd know."

"Like you know any more than I do," he says.

"Hey."

"You don't pay attention," he says. "You think you're just some grown-up version of me or some boy version of Beleza, but you're not."

"Is this your apology?"

"Apology for what," he says, but again he isn't asking a question.

So I just wait.

"I'm not sorry," he says. "My job was to be tasering those things so I was tasering those things."

"I didn't ask you to be *sorry*."

"Okay, then what the hell."

"You don't have to be sorry, Oz. You have to apologize."

"That doesn't make any sense."

"When you hurt someone, you apologize."

"That my lesson of the day?"

"Yes."

He pushes the tip of his thumb into the point of his knife, not hard enough to break the skin, and twists it a little.

"I'm sorry," he says.

"Okay."

"But I'm not, really."

"I know." I close my eyes.

"Beleza says we're supposed to be doing math."

How did I get suckered into being doctor *and* teacher while Beleza gets to sit up there and fish? Maybe I am full of shit thinking that we're partners here and I'm not another one of her charges.

Or maybe she just knows I'm better at math.

I can lie to myself too.

I nod a little and slide to the edge of the bunk so I can sit up. "Okay. Get your book."

SQUISHY SARDINES

"Turkey, Turkey, Turkey!" Zulu jump-spins in circles. "Turkey, Turkey!"

"We are not going to Turkey, my dear," I say.

She points and goes, "THAT'S TURKEY!" as if we can see land and not just more miles and miles and miles of sea, but it is the direction Turkey's in, so at least the kid has something right.

"Hyper child," I say. Beleza looks over from the wheel and grins.

"What's she doing?" she says.

"Being cute."

"Can we play?" says Zoo.

Sure, what the hell. "What do you want to play?"

But she's already sprinted over to Oz, who's eating a can of peaches with his fingers, lying on his back, dripping syrup all over his face. She grabs him, sticky mess and all.

"Oscar, can we play can we play can we play?"

And just because he likes to keep us on our toes, I guess, he sits up, slides the last peach slice down his throat, sets down the can, and says, "Yeah, sure, what the hell."

"Turkey, Turkey, Turkey!"

"So what are we playing?" Beleza says.

"Swab the deck!" Zulu says.

"That's not a game," Beleza says. "That's a chore."

"Turkey!"

"That's a country."

Oscar says, "She gets one more try or I'm going to sleep."

"SQUISHY SARDINES!" Zulu says, immediately, and really, we shouldn't be surprised. Zulu's loved squishy sardines since she was ten months old and we'd carry her around and shove her in places no one else could fit. The game is basically hide-and-seek, but only one person hides and the rest look, and when you find the hiding spot, you have to fit yourself in there with them, until everyone but one person is squished in there, like sardines, I guess, which is even more fitting when you smell like salt and old fish all the time anyway.

"Who's hiding?" I say.

"Belly."

She hops down onto the deck. "Okay. You will regret that decision. No one will ever find me."

"I will find you *first*," Zulu says.

The rest of us close our eyes and count to thirty—switching back and forth every couple numbers between Arabic and Portuguese, like we always do—and then open our eyes and set off looking. Zulu's staring up the mainsail like she's wondering if Bela's in the crow's nest, which I know she isn't because there's no way she'd let Zoo climb up there on her own. "Don't," I tell Zulu.

"Keep your eyes to yourself, *Indi.*"

Oscar's already charged below deck, but I think I would have heard her if she'd gone down the stairs. My best guess is the storage locker near the bow; it's accessed through a little trapdoor, and it's big enough for her to fit in but definitely not big enough for all of us without some serious hilarity, which absolutely is something Beleza would pick. When Beleza aims to have fun, she does it as intensely as she kills monsters.

I make sure Zulu isn't watching me—she's checking around a bunch of nets we have folded by the foremast—before I pull up the hatch and look into the storage locker. Just blankets. I move them around a little, feeling stupid, but she's definitely not there.

When I give up and stand back up, Zulu isn't there either. She must have gone down to the cabin too.

And the thing is, I know it—I know exactly where my siblings are, and it's where they're supposed to be—and it's obviously not as if this is the first time I've been on the deck alone. But I can't help this annoying as hell bubble of panic that comes from them *not being here* when they were *just here*, and it's that kind of codependence that makes me want to run for the hills, in all honesty, to get off at the next port and sprint to town and not look back.

Oscar and Zulu haven't come up from the cabin, so I head down.

Oscar's rooting around the boxes of cereal. "Any sign of them?" I ask, which is a stupid question. If he's out in the open, he clearly doesn't know where they are.

"Nope." He picks up an empty box and looks inside it. "Not in here."

"Ah, shit, that's where I was gonna look."

He grins and drops it. "I'm surprised we can't hear Zoo giggling."

"She found Beleza?"

"Yep. Turned my back and she was gone."

"I'm never going to hear the end of this if you beat me, am I?"

"You better believe it, big brother." He punches me in the shoulder on his way up the stairs. "I'm going to check the storage locker."

"Heh, you do that."

I go through the bathroom, as if there's really any room in there for anyone to hide, and after a while I think I hear footsteps on the stairs. "Oz?" I yell, but he doesn't answer. I come out. "Oz?"

Shit. He totally beat me.

It's just embarrassing at this point, and part of me wants to yell surrender, but then I think of my three siblings all squashed somewhere together, giggling and covering their mouths and having fun and . . . yeah. I'll keep this going a little longer.

Plus, we're not a family that's big on surrendering.

I finally find them, in the ice chest that's been empty since Athens. I open the door and they screech and tumble out and tackle me onto the floor, and they tease me over hugs and kisses and I am laughing so hard it hurts.

RADAR

I'm manning our large radar setup that's kept tucked in the stern of the cabin one night when we're tacking around Skyros. The dozens of islands in the Aegean Sea make sailing through Greece and Turkey a chore, so this is my first break from manning the sails in over twenty hours. To top it all off, the *Salgada* has sprung up a moldy patch near the stern, and if it keeps eating through the deck we're going to be stuck on a sailboat doing an impression of a submarine. The odds of the mold actually progressing that far aren't huge, but it's one more thing to deal with, and it's just been a rough couple of days.

And then the radar blips. Our generator's been soaked a few too many times, so the thing's known for occasionally sending out false signals—as well as shutting down completely at the most inopportune times—but that red dot flashing near the perimeter of the tiny little screen is definitely something. I mess with the gain control to see if it disappears, but even with the sensitivity turned down, the blip's still there. I watch it; it's moving left across the screen, perpendicular to us, which means it's matching our speed but not our course and positioned to collide right into us.

Our old boat, the one we lost with our parents, had a great radar setup that could tell the difference between the electrical transmissions monsters give off—a key way to tell the difference between fish and monsters, by the way, because fish don't literally radiate evil—and radar signals from other ships or weather systems. It's a risky thing, even having radar, because there are monsters we're pretty sure can detect it the same way we detect them, and it's an even more questionable risk when the only indication I have of whether I'm looking at a buoy or a beast with a mouth bigger than our boat is my dubious estimation of a tiny flashing light. Obviously there are tools and measurements to give you a better idea of how close the blip is to you, and how fast it's coming, and those are great when you're tracking a ship with a steady velocity, but not so much when you're worried about a monster that can switch between languishing and sprinting whenever it damn well pleases.

Even over the unrelenting noise of the day—a consequence of sailing against the wind for hours on end—I hear our auxiliary radar up on the deck start screaming. It's just a transmitter that communicates with the big machine down here and shrieks if something is picked up, and a lot of the time when we're all working on the deck or it's too damn hot to be locked down here in the cabin, we're lazy and rely on that. But with all the islands in our area, we have to be much more careful about running right into things, so we're forced to listen to it.

Sure enough, Beleza comes barreling down the stairs, her jacket sweeping over me as she squats next to my chair. "What have we got?"

"You know as much as I do." I pick up our radio mouthpiece. "Should we call?"

She hesitates, for good reason. When we need to alert a ship that they might be about to plow us down, really the only way is to call the nearest island and hope that it's one of their ships, or that they at least know how to contact them. The problem with that is, then that country knows we're out here, and the less attention we can draw to our undocumented ship, radar, and selves, the better.

"What's even closest?" she says.

I check our GPS, then our atlas. "Paros. I think. Maybe Naxos." They're about eight kilometers apart and under a hundred kilometers away from any others. It's not as if we're in the west Mediterranean and can check in with Portugal and Spain and call it a day. "What do you think?"

"Air horn," she says.

"Are you sure?" A nearby boat would hear that, but so would a nearby monster.

She reads my mind, as always. "If it's a monster it's not going to matter."

Because they already know we're here. If we can sense them, they can sense us.

"Okay," I say.

But she's already yelling up the stairs without waiting for my approval. "Oscar! Air horn!"

"What's going on?" Zulu calls from her bunk.

"Get the cannons ready, Zoo."

She sprints up to the deck.

"Is it heading toward us?" Beleza asks.

I shake my head. "Hasn't changed course."

"Could just be a rain cloud."

"Yeah. Maybe."

The air horn blasts from the deck, twice, three times, and Beleza and I stay glued to the screen. The blip continues on its path, not slowing down, not speeding up, not aiming for us, not aiming away from us.

"Scary," I say, before I can stop myself, but Beleza nods, gripping her necklace.

"Update?" Oscar yells.

"One of us should go up to look," I say.

"Yeah," Beleza says, but she doesn't move.

"You want to stay here and keep watch?"

"Yeah."

I stay a minute longer too, and we watch nothing change. Oscar yells down again, and I head up.

"We're okay," I say.

"How sure are you?"

"Not."

He picks up one of the rifles Zulu brought and cocks it. "Right."

Zulu finishes loading the cannons. I sit on a crate and pull her into my lap and wrap her up in one of the damp blankets, and we wait. We stay huddled together for hours, and Oscar stays on edge, and Beleza stays away, while we stare at rain clouds. And nothing else.

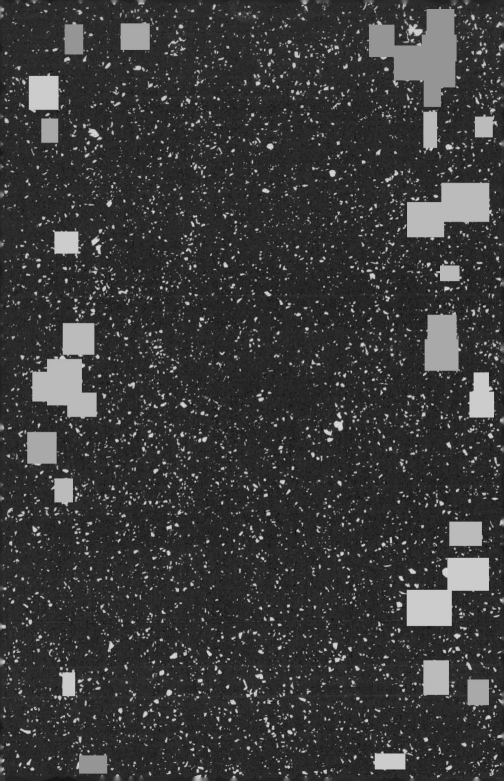

BOSPHORUS

It's time for the trickiest part of our sail to Ukraine. Once we get through the Bosphorus, we're in the Black Sea, and after that it's just a short sail to port. Unfortunately, the Bosphorus is narrow as hell. We already had to navigate the Dardanelles yesterday to get from the Aegean Sea to the Sea of Marmara, and that itself is a tight squeeze, but nothing like this. The Bosphorus is seven hundred meters wide at its narrowest, and we're unannounced, underprepared, and, obviously, underwhelming at detecting other ships that might be trying to use the strait while we are. It's easily the most nerve-racking thing we've done without our parents, hunts possibly included. It doesn't help that Beleza and I are the only ones worrying about it, because, yeah, it's hard to explain to kids why they should be worried about sailing when they know how to spear down dragons.

The wind isn't on our side today either. Beleza's hair is whipping around everywhere while she's trying to decipher a printout of weather patterns our radar gave us, and the sails are putting up a fight, beating against the slides and roaring every time I adjust the line.

"We're going to ram into a cliff," Beleza says.

"Shut up."

"You feeling ready?"

I swallow. The tight turn ahead is one of the Bosphorus's many worst features. "What if I'm not?"

"Then we're going to ram into a cliff."

"Yeah." I know neither of us is dying for me to take the lead on this one, but the fact of the matter is I have five inches and fifty pounds on her.

She comes over and joins me at the wheel. "Okay. We're waiting until we get to nine knots so the turn will be easier."

"That's not too fast?"

"No, you can do it. I'm right here."

It's times like this I wish our boat had a tiller instead of a wheel; the *Salgada*'s a little too big for a tiller, but if we had one I'd get a lot more tactile feedback from the water while I'm steering. My parents taught me to sail on a tiller boat. The fact that I'm not comfortable right now is *their fault*, and I'm angry as suddenly and briefly as an electric shock.

Beleza's too busy ordering around the kids to notice. "Do you want us to tip over?" she asks them. "Stay on *that* side, I told you."

"Zulu's like ten pounds," I say. "It doesn't matter where her weight is."

"It's practice," Beleza says. "Someday it's gonna matter, and now she'll know. You remember learning?"

I nod, not looking at her, and she reaches her hand up and scratches the back of my head for just a second, says, "Okay. You got this, *chico.* Ready about!"

Oscar grabs the mainsail, ready to tack. I take a deep breath.

"LEE-HO!" Beleza calls, and I heave my weight against the wheel.

It's a scary as hell thirty kilometers, but we do it. All by ourselves, we do it. And Beleza wraps herself around my neck and kisses me and tells me how proud she is, and she smiles and pinches my cheek and I would do it again ten times over if my big sister asked me to.

A SURPRISE ARRIVAL

It's been a long time since I was in a place where I really spoke none of the language. As soon as we rise out of the Sea of Azov to port in Mariupol, Oscar ducks into a tourist shop and comes out with a guidebook we apparently all decide to pretend he paid for, even though none of us knows what Ukrainian currency is even called. The guidebook would probably tell us, but it's in English, which is practically as useless. Beleza digs through the moldy pile of wet encyclopedias and romance novels we call a library and comes up with a Spanish-to-English dictionary, so cross-referencing the two will probably be enough to help us suss out street signs and maps at the very least, but we feel pretty stupid for complaining about French right about now.

"Where are we going?" Zulu says.

"Train station." Beleza's using her Mom voice and her Dad assertive-glare-at-the-horizon to show she's not in a mood for chitchat. We're on a bench on the other side of the harbor, the *Salgada* still within view, and she has a map and the guide-book and the dictionary and is trying to figure out how we even get to the station, let alone what train to actually get on and where to get off. All to talk to some guy who probably won't have any information for us. Not that it's information I want anyway. I think I'm supposed to be helping decipher the train, but she has all the materials, and I'm trying to figure out what all this noise is just a couple boats down from us.

Zulu notices it too. She stands on the bench next to Beleza and points. "Oscar, look!"

"*Oscar, look,*" he mocks, but he does.

A ship's coming in, a nice one, better than any we ever had, a little beat-up but *gorgeous*, with two decks and huge portholes and a mermaid figurehead. It's stocked with supplies too, boxes and boxes of sealed-up who-knows stacked on the upper deck. The crew seems infinite. Some of them are arranging the boxes, some are hauling line, some have already disembarked to help guide her in, but they're all yelling at each other in Italian, I think, and everyone around the harbor is rushing to help. If you look like you can tip people, you can get anyone to help you in harbors. If you look like four shabby orphans in a shabby sailboat, you'll be doing the work yourself. Whoever owns that boat has money and everyone knows it.

"Can we go watch?" Zulu says.

"No." Beleza still hasn't looked up. "We don't have time, Zoo. You've seen lots of boats."

"What language is that, Indi?" Zulu says.

"I think Italian."

"*Molto bene!*" Zulu jumps up and down. "*Non parlo Italiano! Avanti!*"

"I'm getting a headache," Oscar grumbles.

"Okay," Beleza says. "I think I've got it."

"We need to get a cab?" I say it mostly for Oscar's benefit. He likes cars, a lot.

But she says, "No. It's not a bad walk."

"You sure?"

"Yeah. Maybe on the other side. I have an address for this guy, but I don't know exactly where the train's going to let off. And we don't have money for a cab now."

"We're going to need to get money exchanged anyway."

"We can do that at the train station." It's her Mom voice again. She's done discussing this.

I mouth *Sorry, buddy* to Oscar. He shrugs.

I go ahead and steer us toward the fancy boat on the way out of the harbor, though, and Beleza doesn't argue. Zulu's so excited, it's the cutest damn thing, bouncing on her toes and telling me all the parts of the ship, making me forget for a minute why I hate all this so much.

And then someone swings off the boat, a blur of bright blue fabric and dark skin and Arabic orders to the crew. I recognize the voice right away.

What the hell, Hura. You've certainly traded up.

WAITING

Between the noise of the crowds and the traffic and the bustle of trying to usher the damn kids from street to street, I don't get to talk to Beleza until we're stepping into the station. Zulu's been shivering for the past few blocks, so Beleza's trying to pull her into a sweater with one hand and organize our (fake) passports with the other. I'd help, but I'm trying to fit all the maps into Bela's too-small bag and straighten Oscar's clothes and my clothes so we look a little less like vagrants the policeman eyeing us will want to throw out.

"I don't think I like that she's here," I say to Beleza.

"What?" she says, distracted still.

"That girl. Did you see her?"

"Indi, what girl. Okay, Zulu, that's better, yeah?"

"Getting off the boat."

"Which boat?"

"She's the girl from the bar back in Marseille," I say. "The one I slept with while you were with that guy Garrison or whatever."

"She's here?"

"That's what I said."

"Zulu, stay with—yeah, I get it, it's cute, you've seen dogs before, you can't just wander—"

"I don't even think that's a dog," Zulu says. "I'm suspicious."

"It's *weird* that she just shows up here," I say to Beleza. "I don't think I like it."

"So don't sleep with her again."

"That's not what I'm saying."

"You think she's hunting you down?" Oscar says. "Were you that bad?"

"No one else is concerned about this?"

"I've got other things on my mind, Indi," Beleza says, and the thing is, if she meant the hyper six-year-old she has by one hand or the twelve-year-old in the other, then maybe I'd be okay with it. Hell, maybe I'd be okay with it if she was talking about getting us on the right train. But she's not, because I *know* her, because I know what it means when she gets *this* snappy, and *this* efficient. All Beleza's thinking about right now is revenge. All she's thinking about is what this guy is going to tell us and how quickly that can lead us to the monster and how cleanly she can lop off its head or burn it to muscle or spear it with poison or whatever it takes. And it's just so damn frustrating, because it's so ephemeral and transient and . . . metaphorical, what she wants, when we are right here, I am her physically present little brother, and we're a million damn miles apart.

And my argument would be so, so much more compelling if I had anything real I needed her to pay attention to instead of a vaguely weird feeling about a vaguely weird girl.

I'm just so tired of arguing. So damn tired of always being on my toes and tracking Beleza's moods to figure out when I can talk to her. I'm sick of the significance and the rhythm and the pacing of everything, sick of having to steer my thoughts and my family like a sail.

I'm so tired.

"I need coffee," I tell her. "I'll get hot chocolate for the kids."

"I'm not a *kid*," Oscar says. "I want coffee." We ignore him.

"Where?" Beleza says, and I point at the little café close to the ticket counter, and she nods and says, "Okay, I'll get the tickets, take—"

"You need them," I say. "You need help with the documents and the translating and stuff."

Please just give me a minute.

"Okay," she says. I think she believes me. I don't think she's reading my mind.

I get by in the shop with counting and pointing and I'm at the counter with two coffees and two hot chocolates when I remember that, after all these discussions of it, I *still* don't have Ukrainian money. It's this kind of small, substantive failure that makes me want to run away and never talk to another person again. God, I spent weeks wishing I could get off our boat and now I wish I were back at sea surrounded by blue and white and *quiet*.

A coffee cup plunks down next to me on the counter, and a hand comes up, offers money, gestures to my things and hers.

"Hi, Hura."

She sips and smiles. "This is quite the surprise, huh!"

"What is?"

"Running into each other?"

"Is it?" I pick up the coffee cups and go for the hot choco-lates, but Hura grabs them before I can. I look over at the ticket counters, but my siblings are still in line, arguing about something. From this distance, it's impossible to tell that they aren't speaking the same language as everyone around us. They're all part of the same noise I don't understand.

And in the middle of it, Hura and me.

She sees where I'm looking. "That's your brother and sister, right?"

"Sisters. The older one's mine too."

"Oh, yeah, she looks like you."

"You think?"

"Absolutely." She looks at me now. "You don't?"

"I look like my dad, she looks like my mom."

"Where are they?"

"Dead."

"Sorry."

I shrug. "Guessing yours are too."

She laughs, and drinks—one of the hot chocolates. Goddamnit. "You don't even know how old I am."

"It is weird."

"Hmm?"

"That you're here. I'm conceding. It's weird."

"Aw, I thought we were going to keep playing."

She's making me nervous, is the thing. "Did you follow us?"

"Don't flatter yourself."

"That's not an answer."

She waves her hand at nothing. "You saw what I came in on. I've been busy with my own shit. Haven't exactly had time to tail you."

"And yet you're here, the same day we're here."

"Guess I'm a faster sailer." She grins. "Or I've just got a better crew."

I watch Beleza grab Zulu and haul her back in line, give her a light tap on the back of her head and then a kiss. "No such thing," I say.

"I don't know. That little one couldn't haul a line like my guys."

"Your guys even have names?"

"Sure. Sailors one through eight."

"Where are you headed next?"

She heaves out a sigh. "Not sure. I don't like the odds of the sailors coming back with me without a fight."

"Ha, fighting with your crew. That one I get." Though I'm not for a second losing sight of the differences between my situation and what I can figure out of hers. She's being glib, sure, but there's nothing glib about being in a strange country with nobody on your side. I watch her open up a packet of biscuits, and stuff a few in her mouth and I don't see any trace of fear in her, or even apprehension, or even anything. "So you're staying here?" I ask her, trying to figure out why she's in Ukraine, of all places.

"Yeah, I think so. Try to find some work."

"Gotta pay your guys."

"Eh, feed them, at least."

"You're kind of awful, aren't you?"

She grins. "And you're going where?"

Beleza's waving me over. "I feel like I shouldn't tell you," I say.

Hura laughs. "Fair enough. Hook up when you get back? You got a cell phone?"

"No."

"How do you even . . ." She shakes her head, laughing a little, and fishes a scrap of paper and a pen out of her bag. She yanks the cap of the pen off with her teeth and writes down a number. "That's mine, if you can find a phone."

"Sure."

"Cool."

Beleza has an eyebrow raised when I get to her. She hands me a ticket. "Made a friend?"

"Shut up, Bela," I say, and for the first time possibly ever, she does.

LOST

"I spy . . ." Zulu looks around, her eyes darting over person after person after person. We're on the platform now, waiting for the train, and it's packed. There are four different platforms and four different trains off from where we're standing, all of them labeled in an alphabet we don't know, let alone language. Oscar begrudgingly has Zulu by the hand, and Beleza has a grip of the hem of my sleeve, just two fingers, like if she's subtle enough I won't notice she's leashing me like our six-year-old.

"What do you spy?" I ask.

"No, I want to play with Oscar!" I'll never understand why she keeps trying to be friends with him when Beleza and I are right here to indulge her. The kid's like me, a glutton for punishment.

Predictably, he says, "Shut up, runt."

"I think we're that one?" Beleza says to me, pointing at a platform.

"That's what I was thinking too. I'm not sure."

"Yeah, me neither. Shit."

"Something *blue*," Zulu insists.

I say, "Zoo, we'll play with you on the train, okay?"

"There might not even be anything blue on the train!"

"It's a whole *train*," Oscar says. "Something's gonna be blue."

"You don't know."

"Pipsqueak."

"Asshole."

"You guys," Beleza says. "Can you please, for one minute in your entire stupid lives, shut the hell up?"

They both mutter, "Fine," in unison, both in Portuguese—a very, very rare case of them doing something together, and of course it's accidental.

There's an announcement over the speakers, spoken so fast that I can't believe even people who speak Ukrainian could follow. But the rush of movement around us, people jostling us on top of each other and away from each other somehow at the same time, reminds me again that we're alone, that we're the only ones who don't understand. My brother, my sisters, and me. Our own little messed-up country.

I wonder where Hura is now.

"Come on," Beleza says, pointing to a train pulling up.

"Are you sure?" I say.

"No. Come on." And of course after that she's running. I grab Oscar's shirt and pull him along after me, and I feel him stumble but I don't look back, because all of a sudden the idea of being separated from Beleza is the scariest thing I can imagine.

Sometimes I would trade all of the little nothing I have just to know what it is I really want.

I scramble onto the train and hitch my falling backpack over my shoulder about a second before it would have slipped into the gap between the train and the platform. God, I need to be more careful. I could have lost our journal.

"I hurt myself," Oscar mumbles. I turn around and yeah, he's got a hole in the knee of his jeans and a bloody knee peeking through.

"Ouch," I say. "I'll fix it once we're sitting." We can't look for a compartment yet because business people and mothers with hordes of kids even more unruly than mine are pushing past us with their shoulders and their suitcases. The train starts to roll, and I grab onto a nearby pole before I fall over. A sailor without sea legs.

The crowd clears enough that I can finally see all of Beleza and not just a hint of her stringy hair, and she says in mostly-Arabic, "Come on, let's find . . . anywhere. Once people start to smell us they'll give us space to ourselves."

"I still don't think we're going to get four seats," I say.

"Three's fine, we can hold Zoo on—"

She freezes, and all three of us realize it at the same time.

We don't have Zulu.

We're a flurry of overlapping words and actions, pushing our way into a compartment to press against the window—*I thought you had her!*—craning our necks to try to see back to the station as the train picks up speed—*They have to turn the train around!*—crying, *There has to be someone here who speaks*...

And then that tiny voice from the end of the car. "Belly!" It's her.

She looks scared out of her damn mind. She must have gotten pushed along and tangled up in some other family. For a second, someone probably thought our baby belonged to them.

It's Oscar who gets to her first, who drops to his knees in front of her and gathers her up and pushes his face into her hair and sobs.

SPIT

Once Oscar and Zulu have fallen asleep on top of each other against the train window, Beleza shifts Zulu's hip off her leg and produces a deck of cards from one of the thousands of pockets of her coat. She deals out half to me and we play Spit for a while.

"So this guy knew Mom and Dad?" I say, almost whispering, even though the kids regularly sleep through thunderstorms, and even if everyone on this train wasn't bellowing at each other I doubt any of them speak Portuguese.

But I'm quiet anyway.

She nods and licks her finger to pick up a card. "The guy in Marseille said they had a run-in less than a year ago. The Ukrainian guy called him telling him about this reckless sic couple he practically had to pull out of something's mouth."

"That has to be them."

"Best lead we've got so far, at least." She flicks her eyes up to me. "They were good at what they did."

We used to criticize them together, sometimes just in that *Oh my God parents are the worst* way, but also when we were exhausted down to our lungs, when we were bruised to all hell, when we watched over the little kids because our parents were too busy writing in the damn notebook. We used to do that together.

Now Beleza just takes her gaze off me so quickly and looks out the window. In profile she looks very young, for a second.

"What river is this?" she says. I guess we're not playing cards anymore.

I know the word *river* in English—I know just about every water-related word in most languages—so it isn't too hard to find the section in the guidebook. I flip through the Spanish-English dictionary until I get the word *southern* and scan the guidebook page until I find it.

"Pivdennyl Buh," I attempt to say, and this time I'm being quiet because I'm not really in the mood to have strangers laugh at my terrible attempts at Ukrainian. I turn the guide-book around so she can see it. "Check out the bridge."

She smiles. "Huge."

"Yeah."

"It really is wherever you go, huh?" She touches the window glass really lightly, like she doesn't know she's doing it.

"Water?"

"Mmm-hmm."

"Yeah. Can't get away from it."

"Kind of like a grouchy little brother," she says, trapping

my foot between hers, grinning up at me. Making a peace offering.

"What are you talking about? Your grouchy little brother's asleep," I say, just to keep things from getting too mushy.

"I love you," she says, to ruin that.

I pretend to read something in the guidebook with some magically developed English knowledge before I mumble, "Loveyoutoo."

"You know I'd kill for you to be happy, right?"

I don't look up. "The irony is that killing is what makes me unhappy."

"Indi . . ."

"What?" There's really nothing she can say to that, is the thing.

But she says, "We're saving the world, you know."

It's not the first time someone's pulled that on me—used to be my parents—but I still don't know how to respond to it. She puts two fingers under my chin to lift up my head and nods toward the window, and I look out over flat country-side with houses way in the distance, at the sun blaring like a spotlight on the roofs, and just a bit of the river snaking ahead of us.

I do think it's the first time someone's said it to me when the world didn't just look like gray-blue nothingness.

"It's a nice world," I say, softly.

"Uh-huh."

My eyes are wet suddenly, and I squeeze them shut. She scratches at my knee a little, waiting.

"I want to be in it so bad," I whisper.

INDUSTRY

The train lets us off hours later in Donetsk, at which point I'd translated enough of the guidebook to know that it's an industrial city on a completely different river than the one we rode past, and that it's made up of gorgeous gold towers and monuments. The guidebook is full of glossy pictures of pure-white stone obelisks that remind me of Morocco. But as soon as we get off the train, Oscar limping a little on his torn-up knee, Zulu asleep on Beleza's back, it's clear that the guidebook is out of date. Maybe a hundred years out of date.

This place is a rubble city. We walk out of the station and nearly trip over a statue that's been leveled down to my knees. It's dusty here, and hundreds and hundreds of people are streaming past us each minute, the guys in backpacks and boots and hair gel and the girls in all-black with white hair and tottery high heels, and none of them looks distressed.

There's a population of almost a million right in the city, the guidebook said, and another two million in the surrounding area, but it feels like so many more. I wonder how outdated this guidebook can really be, because I can't conceptualize that many people living in one place, and it can't be more now. That can't have changed. How do you attract that many people and keep them here, when your city is rubble?

Beleza tugs my elbow. "How much money do we have?"

"I don't know."

"We should see if we can spring for a sleeper car tonight," she says. "When we head back to Mariupul."

"We can't just get a place here overnight?"

She shifts Zulu off her back and onto mine. A practiced move. "Why waste time?"

I don't say anything because . . . well. Why waste time.

Bela has a shoddy piece of paper with shoddy bits of directions on it that she got from the retired sic back in Marseille. We turn down streets, matching up the shapes of the letters on the street signs with the shapes on the paper. Unlike the guidebook, that guy seemed to know what the place looks like now.

"Damn," Beleza breathes at one point.

"We lost?" I snatch Oscar by the sleeve as he starts to wander away to Lord knows what. That kid could find a distraction in an empty room.

"No," she says. "Just . . ." She shrugs. "This is what the island looked like."

"Oh."

Another shrug. "But without the people."

THE ISLAND

—is not something I know much about.

It's a small island close to Portugal. For all intents and purposes, there's nothing left of it. A few square miles of a kind of rubble. My mother was born there, and my father was a commercial sailor who turned a temporary stay into an illegal permanent one just two days after he met my mother. They lived in Mom's parents' house, and when her mother and father both died, they stayed. The house was on the very, very northern edge of the island. It was the farthest house up because my mom's dad built it there himself because that was where he liked the view the most. It's just trivial shit like that, and all of a sudden you've created your whole life.

Because the monster just happened to attack from the southern side. My parents had been in that house for ten years. Beleza was about two.

And that day my parents, my parents and Bela, became part of the tiny little group that survived an attack from these creatures they'd never known existed.

There's a word for people like that, and it's *sics.*

And then they got a clipper and another clipper and they got the *Salgada* and they got the ship they went down on. And the whole time they just kept having babies.

And here we are.

OF THE STATE

"Earthquake," Chester La Manza says. "Or at least that's what they're calling it. City looked a lot different before a few *earthquakes*." He holds up the whistling teakettle. "How many cups?"

La Manza speaks Spanish, thank God, and was either expecting us or is very laid-back about surprise visitors. At the very least, he knew our names from his friend back in Marseille. His apartment is high up in a building, small and cluttered, mostly with newspapers and half-drained tea mugs. Oscar's playing with the microwave, setting it for a few seconds, letting it beep, opening it, setting it again. The fact that La Manza hasn't killed him already says enough about his character for me to feel comfortable.

"Just one for Indi," Beleza says.

La Manza nods and pours. "You know, you look just like your mother."

"You knew our mother?" I say, and add a quick *Thank you* when he hands me the cup. We'll all drink tea when it's freezing and pouring rain in the middle of the ocean, but I'm the only one who actually likes it. Better with whiskey, but it seems early to ask this guy for that.

"Are you another . . . retired guy?" Beleza asks. Our Spanish isn't anything special.

He coughs out a laugh. "Please. Like you can retire in this world."

She's beaming. I think she wants to marry the old bastard.

He pulls up his shirtsleeve to reveal a brace on his left wrist. "Waiting on this thing before I go out again."

She curls up on the couch like she belongs here. "What happened?"

"Darkrider." Big beasties. Known for ferrying smaller ones around on their backs, just to be scarier. I don't think it even benefits them. I think it's actually just to be scary.

"Ooooh," Beleza says.

"All by myself."

She gapes. "No way."

He grins.

"That must have been *amazing.*"

"What happened to your wrist?" Oscar says. "Did the bone show?" He's even distracted from the microwave.

"Oscar," I say.

"Hey," Oscar says. "You're a doctor. You should *love* it when the bone shows."

I'm getting caught up in this against my will, but I'm not nearly as far gone as they are, hanging on La Manza's every word, envisioning being in that fight so vividly I can almost see it right through their eyes.

Zulu, on the other hand, is still kneeling on the windowsill. "Indi?"

"Yeah?"

"If I dropped something on someone from this high up, would they die?"

And she was my last hope for normalcy. But I'm laughing around my tea; I can't help it.

La Manza starts to clear away some newspapers from the coffee table, then gives up, shrugs, and sits right on top of them. "So you four are looking for it?"

"It took down our parents," Beleza says. "Gotta finish what they started."

And then what.

Beleza holds out her hand to me without looking my way and I hand her our parents' journal. She flips to the parts we've dog-eared and shows him. "But we don't know the name."

He raises his eyebrows. "You don't know the name? Thought you were sics born and bred."

She scowls at him.

He laughs. "This thing's a legend. Come with me." He waves us down the hallway, and I whistle at Oscar and Zulu to look alive and follow us.

He takes us to a room wallpapered with articles and sketches. He's not nearly the artist our father was. "Here," he says. There's a whole corner devoted to this thing. Mysterious sinkholes taking down whole fleets. Harems of monk seals there one day and gone the next. And then notes written by us, people who know better, in Spanish, Italian, Greek: *Strikes again. Might be another sighting? Howling heard near Biscayne Bay.*

"They call it El Diamante," La Manza says. "Got these eyes like uncarved diamonds. That's the legend, anyway. Only heard of a few people who saw it and lived, and that's just because they were smart enough and lucky enough to avoid a fight."

"Oscar," I say quietly.

"What?"

I point my chin to Zulu. "Take her outside."

"Why?"

"She doesn't need to hear all this."

"You do it."

"Oscar."

"I need to hear it more than you do!"

"That doesn't make any damn sense. Take your sister outside."

He groans, then drags Zulu out while she shrieks.

"What do you know about killing it?" Beleza says.

La Manza just raises an eyebrow at her. She crosses her arms.

"Aren't you a little small?" he says.

"Hey," I say.

Beleza nods toward me. "He's big."

It's easier than arguing. We're used to this shit.

He sizes me up and nods a little, but says, "Doesn't matter. You could be eight feet tall and ten feet wide and you still shouldn't be getting involved with El Diamante." He taps one of the pictures. "Could swallow up whole buildings if it could get on land. Last spotted near Turkey, far as I know. I've had three other sics coming in about this thing in the last two months alone," he says, "and I'm not exactly a high-traffic destination. I bet if you ask someone who's got more of a reputation than me, he'll tell you—"

"Or *she'll* tell you," I mumble in Arabic, and Beleza winks at me.

"—that they're coming in every week. You're not the only ones with a bone to pick here. You heard of the Vasquezes?"

"Of course," I say. Big-time sics. Took down a whole herd of tightwinders once. Cut through the coils ten at a time with razor-wire nets. Ingenious.

"Dead," he says.

"What?"

"Went after the thing and went down a couple weeks ago," he says. "Which means now you've got a dozen more ships full of *their* relatives going after it for revenge." He blows out a mouthful of air. "I'll tell you, for people who die all the time, our line of work really doesn't know how to let go. You want my advice?"

"At this point? Not particularly," Beleza says.

"Stick to your cat-eaters," he says. "Do some commercial fishing, get older, get some meat on your bones. And work your way up to something bigger. Something that's a hell of a lot smaller than El Diamante."

CIVILIZATION AND STUFF

"So what now?" I say as we get off the train, Oscar and I hauling our bags over our shoulders, Beleza corralling a sleepy-headed Zulu. Who the hell knows what the plan is now that Bela's revenge mission is clearly off the table.

"Head toward Turkey," she says. "We could easily get through the Bosphorus before dark."

"Or we could stay around here for a few days."

She wrinkles her nose. "Why?"

"There's like, you know. Civilization and stuff." A guy running for his train shoulder-checks me and almost knocks me over. Oscar tries to kick him in the shin on my behalf, but he's gone too fast.

"Oh, yeah," Beleza says. "Civilization's the best."

"Can we take a cab?" Oscar says.

Zulu says, "Yeah, yeah, yeah, can we?"

"Yeah," I say, just because I knew Beleza was going to say no, and I don't need her opinion on every damn discussion, no matter what she might believe. I don't know if it's because she's older or if it's because she was born before ship life and she thinks that means something.

We get into the cab in some semblance of a mutual silent treatment, each of us only making eye contact accidentally over the kids' heads while we're shepherding them around. They're hopping up like popcorn every second and a half, stomping on our laps and feet when they leap to look out the windows and see something that fits one of the five Ukrainian words they've picked up since we floated into town. "*Gray! Bird! Good morning, madam!*"

"It's ten at night and that was a guy," Beleza says.

I clear my throat. "So . . . why are we in such a hurry to get back out there—we got a job or something?"

"A job?" Oscar says. "Money?"

"When do you two think I heard about some other job?" Beleza grouches. She slumps back in her seat and looks very young for a moment. "You two have been attached to me all day."

"Three," Zulu contributes.

"Besides," Beleza says to Oscar. "What do you even need money for, you little shit, you steal anything that doesn't run away too fast." She pauses. "Though I probably shouldn't be on you about stealing right now." She pulls a piece of paper out of her bra. "Ta-da!"

I snatch it away. It's coordinates, a whole collection of them, and a small monster sketch. I saw it pinned on La

Manza's wall, on his little El Diamante shrine.

And I guess I'm really stupid, because I didn't realize until this second how *entirely* different Beleza and I felt about that meeting. We can't go after that thing.

"Bela, we can't."

"Can't what?" Oscar says. Now he snatches the paper. "Aw, hell yeah!" He high-fives Beleza.

"We should go after the treasure instead," I say, flicking her necklace.

"You ever think about the treasure?"

She ignores me.

"You shouldn't have taken this," I say.

She shrugs. "You took his tea."

"Wow, I took a cup of tea that he offered, that's the same."

"You stole two boxes and put them in your backpack."

Damn. "Well . . . it was really good," I say.

She laughs.

"Plus I was raised by a fucking thief," I say. I drop my head on her shoulder without really meaning to. I don't understand myself. I'm so mad at her and so amazed at her and so tired.

She pats my head. "And don't you forget it."

"We're not going after that thing," I say, my eyes closed.

Pat pat pat. "Sure we are."

DETOUR

I kick the pieces of the broken stove that for some reason we still haven't moved out of the way of the bathroom door so I can get it closed. It's still too cramped in this damn ship to get it completely shut, but I can shove it so it gets jammed into the swollen wood of the doorframe and would need a good slam to get knocked loose. Hopefully that's enough of a "do not disturb" signal if any of my siblings end up below deck.

I barely have my pants unzipped when I hear boots coming down the stairs, so heavy-stepped it can only be Oscar.

"Indi! Where are you?" he yells. In Turkish, for some reason.

I've opened a magazine, but damn it, I'm paying enough attention to Oscar to figure out what language he's speaking. I wish I could close my ears like eyes.

"Indi! Beleza wants you to count how many canvas patches we have left!" Arabic now. We don't know all that much Turkish.

Damn it!

I'm about to give up and stuff myself back in but then Oscar yells, "I think he's in the head," and then clomps up to the deck. Thank God. I open the magazine to a new page—

"Hey Indi!"

—and slam it shut again. High-heeled boots this time.

"Hurry it up in there, all right? I want to get dinner started before we go."

"I want *real food*!" Zulu shrieks from the deck, and Beleza grumbles something and heads back up the stairs to deal with her.

I get about three minutes this time—almost enough time to get my siblings' voices out of my head so I can think about the girl in this magazine or a girl I met once in India or that guy with amazing hands back in Côte d'Ivoire or *literally anything but them*—before there's banging on the door out of nowhere and Zulu's oh-so-charming whine: "Indi! I have to *go*!"

"I'm not doing all this work by myself!" Oscar yells.

"Indi, open the door before Zulu pees herself."

"I'm not going to—"

I zip up and tear the door open and shove everyone out of the way and nearly break my neck on the broken stove pieces. "We can leave tomorrow," I say in my best imitation of Dad's *not messing around* voice. "I'm going out."

Beleza opens her mouth like she's going to argue and then looks at the magazine on the floor and laughs. "Have a good time, champ."

I hate my life.

HER AGAIN

Hura and I share a pack of cigarettes on the roof of the dilap-
idated Ukrainian house we just commandeered for two hours.
We're looking into windows of office buildings and run-down
hotels, watching ships float out of the harbor. She takes a pull
on a cigarette, hands it to me, stretches out on her back.

"So can I ask you something?" she says.

"Sure."

"What's this?"

I look. She's got my parents' notebook.

"Whoa." I reach for it, and she pulls it away just barely,
taunting me. "Where did you get that?" I say.

"Uh, your jacket, where do you think?"

"What'd you go through my jacket for?" I make a grab for it
again, and this time she lets me take it.

"Condom? Remember?"

"Right."

"Made for some light reading after you passed out," she says.

My parents drilled into me my entire life not to let lubs—even seafaring-not-really-lubs like this girl—know about monsters. They'll just think you're crazy, or go after them themselves and get hurt. They'll call the police and have you taken away from your delusional family. They'll laugh at you. *Do you want people to laugh at you, Indi?*

She frowns, looking at me. "Relax, I could barely read any of it. What language is this in, anyway?"

"Portuguese."

"Hopefully your Portuguese is better than your Arabic."

I'm flipping through the notebook, checking to see if any of the clipped-in pages are missing. If there are any photographs stuck in the pages—sometimes there are, before we lose them. Pictures of things we've killed, or Zulu with some kind of tentacle in her mouth, or our parents looking proud of us. But either there weren't any in here or she took them.

"My Arabic's fine."

"If you say so." She's quiet for five seconds, maybe. "So, monsters, huh?"

My insides feel very literally cold. "What?"

"The *drawings* weren't in Portuguese. What is that, some story you're working on?"

"It's my parents'." I can't remember if I told her that my parents were dead, but the way she's looking at me makes me think I must have. Or else she just assumes. I wonder if she has parents. I wonder if before right this second she'd thought about me having parents.

That's stupid. She knows about my sisters and my brother. She knows I have a family.

She knows I have a family and she knows about monsters. Well, she knows everything, then. That's about all there is to me.

And I don't know a thing about her.

"Who's it for?" she says. "The little one? Like a bedtime story?"

"Not exactly."

Why didn't I just say yes? Why didn't I say *Yeah, it's mine, I'm writing a book* or something?

Do I want to tell her?

Oh, God. I want to tell her. I want to tell her I'm about to sail out of here to track down a monster we have no idea how to fight. I want to tell her that Bela's leading us on a revenge mission. I want to tell her how goddamn angry I am.

I want to tell her that I think I'm going to die really soon.

And I'm not really living that life where I have anything to lose anymore from people finding out. What are they going to do, take me away from Beleza?

Like anyone could.

Like I would blame anyone for trying.

"My parents . . . my sister," I say. "My sister and I. We fight these."

"Fight what?"

I gesture toward the notebook. "All of it. We find them and kill them."

She's quiet for just a few seconds. "Why?"

"What?"

"Why do you kill them?"

Well, that isn't what I was expecting.

"Because . . . they're monsters," I say.

"Okay, but how are we, you know, defining monsters. Do you kill sharks?"

"Sharks are nothing. They're just fish."

"So these things aren't fish?"

I take the notebook from her and flip through until I find a drawing of a morde d'eau. "We took down one of *these* a few weeks ago, right before we ported in France. You look at that and tell me it's a fish."

She stares at the picture, then breathes out. "Huh."

"What?"

"I've seen this."

"What?"

"I saw this thing. About a month ago. Near Algeria. That must have been right before you killed it, right?"

"Or it was another one."

"There are multiples of each one?"

"Yeah. Except . . . here." I turn to the El Diamante section. "Everyone says there's only one of these."

"Well, it had to have *parents*."

"There are reports of this thing going back centuries," I say. "It's this huge, legendary thing. Most of them aren't like that. Most of them are just—"

"Fish?"

"They're not fish!"

"You're basically a fisherman."

"Shut up." I tug on her sleeve, and she turns and rests her forehead against my neck a little bit, and we just sit there, watching a ship pull out of the harbor. Her skin is cool on my collarbone, and her fingers make a circle around my wrist.

"We think that's what killed my parents," I say.

"That legendary thing?"

"El Diamante. Yeah."

"Why do you think that?"

I shrug, dislodging her. "Nothing else could have taken them down," I say. "They were incredible." And then I swallow and swallow and swallow.

"Yeah?" she says, gently.

"You should see all the stuff we have. Weapons, all this radar tech. Half of it you can't get anywhere, my parents just built it. Their ship was way better and we still have a ton."

"Hmm."

"What?"

"El Diamante, did you say?"

"What? Yeah."

"I think I heard something about that," she says. "I didn't know what it meant at the time. But I definitely heard someone say *almaz* when I was in this tavern last night."

"*Almaz?*"

"Ukrainian for *diamond*. And he was some ragged old sailor. Talking to this whole group of gaping baby sailors."

"You speak Ukrainian?"

She shrugs. "Enough to know he said he'd seen it close by."

"Give me the address of that tavern," I say.

DIVERSION

The kids are starving and we have a little more Ukrainian money to burn off, so Beleza and I leave them at a café close to the harbor while we make the two-mile walk to the tavern.

"You think they know how to ask to use the phone if they need to?" Beleza says.

"They can gesture."

"I guess. And who do they have to call, anyway? When did we become their worried parents?" she says. "The ship's right there if they need it. They're fine."

"I did."

"What?"

"I became their worried parent. Parents."

She slows down. Doesn't stop. "What are you talking about?"

"I watch them, I stitch them up, I make sure they do their chores and go to sleep and are fed and clean and healthy. All you do is . . ."

She still hasn't stopped. "All I do is make sure they don't get eaten by monsters."

"Yeah."

"Well, that's the damn world we're in, Indi."

"It's not the only world."

"There's nothing real out there to be scared of," she says. "Nothing but monsters and pirates."

"Look, you were the one who started worrying about them right now, with no monsters and no pirates."

"Yeah, well, I love them. Is that so hard to keep in mind?"

"You tell me."

"Screw you, Indi," she says. We keep walking.

/

"This is three-four-eight," Beleza says, pointing at a bicycle repair shop across the street from us. "And that's three-four-nine. Market or something."

"Maybe she meant three-four-six?"

"There is no three-four-six. There aren't any pubs on this whole block, look." Beleza balls the paper up in her hand. "Indi, who the hell is this girl?"

Now she cares. Now that the lead didn't check out, now she cares.

She probably never would have asked otherwise. She doesn't worry about who I'm with or care about who I know.

"She's just my friend," I say.

"Friend," she grumbles. We're speaking Arabic, and she drops the word—*sadiq*—like it's filthy.

"Just because it's basically impossible for me to have a friend doesn't mean I can't—"

"Is she stupid?"

"Beleza, what? No, she's not stupid."

"Then she set us up on purpose."

"What are you talking about?"

"Indi! She sends us on a two-mile walk to some residential nowhere. . . . What code name was she using?"

"Um . . ."

"Her code name, Indi. Was she looking for her own intel or was she here to help? Belasco? Santino?"

"She wasn't . . ."

"She's probably going after El Diamante right now," Beleza says. "She's probably stealing our hunt because you told her too much and she wanted to get us out of the way so she could—"

"That's not it," I say. "She's not a sic."

"She's *what*?"

My sister is looking at me like I am the most unbelievable scum of the unbelievable earth.

"She's not a sic," I say, softly.

"So what is she?"

"She's . . ."

"Oh, God." Beleza presses her hand to her forehead. "Oh, God, she's going to take the kids."

"What? No, no . . ."

"She thinks we're crazy people who hallucinate sea monsters and she knew we wouldn't drag the kids with us so she waited and she's going to take them because she thinks we can't take care of them. . . ."

"No, okay? No, no, no." I put my hands on her shoulders. It's so easy to forget, when I'm not touching her, just how much bigger than her I am. "Look at me."

She does.

"She wouldn't do that," I say. "She doesn't think that way, she's not like that."

"You don't *know* that."

"I do know that! I do actually know some things, Beleza!"

"Stop yelling at me."

I do. "No one is going to take those kids away," I say. "No one's ever going to take those kids from me."

From us, she wants to say. *From us.*

But she doesn't.

It's just too hard to pretend we're in anything together anymore.

But we're running together, at the very least. Running so fast, back to the café where we left the kids, so fast that my legs are burning from my ankles all the way up my thighs. We're practically knocking over old ladies. Practically bowling over kids. Other people's kids.

Because it's been drilled into me for as long as I can remember, since long, long before my parents died: *Watch out for the kids, take care of the kids, teach the kids how to kill, how to read, how to survive.* It crushes me and it has never crushed me like it does right at this moment. And a part of me—a part way, way bigger than it should be, than a good person is allowed to have—wants to keep running all the way past that café, past the harbor, past everything I've ever felt and everything I've been forced to feel and never look back.

But I don't.

They're right there, sitting at a rusty table outside the tiny café. They have a whole collection of straws and mauled straw wrappers between them and are blowing the paper ends at each other. Beleza gathers up Zoo, kisses her, and I ruffle Oscar's hair.

"Hey, kid," I say.

"Hey. What'd you guys find out?"

Bela and I just look at each other.

"Not much," she says. "Let's get back to the ship, okay? Let's get out of here."

Oscar just about leaps out of his seat. "Ready when you are," he says, and then stands there impatiently, like Bela and me, while Zulu painstakingly counts out the money they owe kopiyok by kopiyok and leaves it on the bill.

Once she's finally done, I haul her onto my back and she kicks at Oscar's shoulder all the way to the dock, where Beleza stops so short that I collide with her.

"What the . . . ," she says, and I look up at the *Salgada* and my stomach goes cold.

"Where's our sail?" Zulu says.

"Oh, God," Beleza says.

I say, "No, wait, what if someone's still on there?" She turns and looks at me and her eyes are flashing. "You stay *right* there and keep track of those kids. For once." And then she's sprinting right up onto the ship.

Damn it. Damn it.

It's a full scary silent minute before she reappears at the top of the dock. Her face is flushed. "It's gone." We scramble up onto the deck, and it's immediately clear that it's not just our sail that's missing. Our weapons are gone. Our harpoon guns, our harnesses, our bayonets, tasers. Our blankets. Our stove. All our food.

The little crates Zulu sits on to watch dolphins.

All gone.

I'm staring at our naked beds when Beleza storms down the stairs. "*She* did this, didn't she?"

"I . . ."

"Indi, *who is this girl?*"

"She's a pirate," I say.

STALEMATE

Beleza doesn't say a word to me for four days.

Silent treatments are her specialty, ever since we were kids and we'd argue about whose turn it was to man the boom vang, and she's always been good at it. She'd hold out for ages. I'd wake up in the morning, way past being mad, and talk to her for a whole monologue before I realized she wasn't responding.

It's never been like this, though.

Mostly because I'm pretty sure this is the loudest silent treatment anyone's ever attempted. She screams at the kids, stomps around on the deck, charges up and down the stairs, squeaks the ropes, trying to get the ship back into shape. The kids and I stay out of her way—neither of us has explained Hura to them, and they have finally given up asking—and we run through the money pretty fast just trying to keep them fed. Beleza, as far as I know, doesn't eat. I don't care. I don't care.

On day four she wakes me up with a kick to my wooden slab of a bed. "I got us a job," she says.

I stare at her until I feel like I can speak without screaming. "We don't have a sail," I say. "We don't have weapons. We can't take a *job*, are you insane?"

She looks at me like I'm a cut-up mess of a monster. "We're washing dishes at a café," she says. "What the hell do you think I am? Some revenge-driven maniac?"

"You said it, not me."

"Like I'm going to take shit from the slut with the pirate girlfriend."

"Screw you."

"We start work at five," she says.

"You couldn't get us separate shifts?"

"Trust me," she says. "I tried."

/

I'm pretty sure I'm a better dishwasher than I ever was a sic. Makes sense. I've been cleaning up after my family my whole life—their rotted clothes, cut-open legs, nightmares.

Then again, I've been slaying monsters my whole life too. But it's not like this is the first time I've realized I'm not born to be a hero.

Beleza, on the other hand, is stir-crazy four hours into our first shift. She looks childish in her hairnet and apron, slapping at the bubbles in the sink like she thinks that's going to get the plates clean.

"Cut it out," I hiss at her. "You're going to get us fired."

"No one's even watching us," she says. Which is true—the kitchen's bustling, people yelling at each other in Ukrainian and slamming coffee cups around, and no one's very interested in the teenagers who speak ten words of their language. I don't know how Bela got us this job, except that the wage they're paying us can't possibly be legal. When Beleza told me what we were getting, I could tell by the look on her face that I should just pretend I haven't learned anything about conversion rates by now.

It's going to take us forever to get enough money to buy even bare-bones supplies.

Hmm. Maybe I should let her get us fired. Except that our clothes are literally falling apart, and we're all losing weight, and I don't know who the hell Beleza's going to turn into if she has to stay on land for more than a couple weeks. I'm not sure she ever has.

"Here." I splash her. "Water."

She sighs happily. "Not salty enough."

I look around the kitchen. "I could fix that."

"Now who's gonna get us fired!" She's laughing. I can't remember the last time I made her laugh.

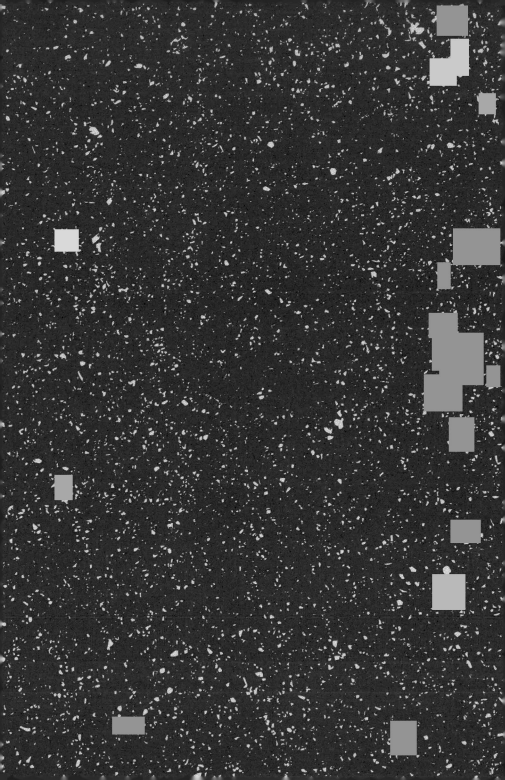

OSCAR

"I'm going insane," Oscar says. "You can't keep doing this to me."

"Do you know what a nightmare you were when you were her age?" I'm putting away the canned food we've bought over the past few days, trying to find an arrangement that will make it look more bountiful than it is.

"Uh, I was awesome."

"You were a terror. Zoo's a sweet little girl."

"She's a *demon*! She never sits still and she always wants to sleep on my bed with me and she's so *cold* and she kicks me and then she screams at the top of her freaking lungs every time she has a nightmare and then she's like, *Oscar I'm hungry* and I'm like, *We're all hungry.*"

I throw a can of green beans at him.

He catches it easily. "Seriously," he says. "Let me come work with you guys."

"No one's going to hire a kid."

"Screw you." He wavers a little before he sits down on the bottom bunk.

"You okay?"

He waves a hand at me and lies down. "I'd be better if you'd just let me steal what we need and we could get out of here."

"Yeah, good luck smuggling a sail under your shirt."

"I could do it."

He probably could. This kid's some kind of thieving savant.

All the more reason to keep him on the boat with Zulu whenever we're not around. It's not like we're feeling too positive about thieves lately.

Or pirates.

I think a part of me knew from the moment I met her. Or at least when she pulled into the harbor on that decked-out ship.

She was just . . . she was too much, that girl, speaking Arabic in her purple dress, pouring water down herself, knowing about monsters, listening to me. . . . It was too much, talking too fast, laughing too much, watching me too closely. It was too much. She was too much.

God, being a pirate must be awesome.

I don't know if I actually think that. It's not like I can say it to anyone and see how it sounds. Oscar would probably take it as inspiration or something. Beleza would possibly actually kill me. Zulu would start singing "A Pirate's Life for Me," and then Beleza would kill *her*.

So I just lie in my bed at night and don't think about her, don't think about her, and think about her.

I sit down next to Oscar on the bunk and slap him on the cheek a few times to get his temperature. "You've got a fever."

"Gross, don't touch me."

"Did you tell Bela?"

"No." He flops onto his back. "This is your job. Fix it."

"Without touching you."

"Yeah."

I scratch the bottom of his foot and he snort-giggles and pulls his knee up to his chest.

"I hate you," he says.

"I'll get you some aspirin."

"Okay. Thanks, Indi."

On the deck, Zulu's swabbing while Beleza polishes one of our brand-new guns. She holds it up to me. "What do you think?"

"Oh, man, let me see that." It's heavy for a handgun, with a wooden handle that has flowers carved in. "This thing's gotta be ancient."

"How cool, right?"

"It's . . . seriously awesome." I turn it over a few times before I hand it back. "Nice find."

"The market has good stuff every once in a while. All we really need is a sail and we'll be ready to go out."

"You're kidding, right?"

"Yay, ready to go!" Zulu says.

Beleza points at her, eyebrows raised at me. "Yay. Ready to go."

"And besides this gun, we have . . . what, to defend ourselves exactly?"

"Hey, you said yourself it's a pretty cool gun."

"Oscar's sick."

"Good *riddance*," Zulu says.

Bela says, "Zoo, are you swabbing?"

"*Yes.*"

"Doesn't look like swabbing."

"*You* don't look like swabbing," she grumbles, and shoves the mop around some so it looks like she's working. Beleza rolls her eyes and goes back to the gun.

"How bad?" she says.

"What?"

"Oscar. How bad?"

"I don't know. He's got a fever."

"Got any cuts that could be infected, anything like that?"

"I don't think so."

"Well, he'll be fine then." She's not even looking up.

"Did you get medicine at the market?"

"What? No."

"No aspirin or anything?"

"I'll get it next time."

I chew on the inside of my lip for a few moments until I'm ready to talk. "We have work in half an hour."

"Fine." She wipes her hands on her pants. "Don't stop, Zulu."

SAIL

Beleza's boots charge down the stairs. I'm shushing her before I can even see her face, but she ignores me and holds up a folded-up sail, grinning, and gives a whoop of celebration.

"Cool," I say.

"Check it out!"

"*Shhh*. He's sleeping." I had to quit work early to check on Oscar. I thought Beleza would insist on being the one to leave, but I guess she's gotten used to coming home with money. And supplies.

"What'd you get?" Zulu says. She's on the top bunk, playing with these two ragged dolls Oscar stole for her a few towns back.

"We got a sail!" Beleza says. "We're going to be out of here before we know it, which is good because—"

"Beleza," I say. "Come on."

She heaves this big sigh, but actually puts the sail down and kneels next to the bunk. "How's he doing?"

"Better than yesterday, I think. Only threw up a few times. At least I got him to sleep."

"Poor little bug."

"Yeah. We might want to get him to a real doctor soon."

"That's what *you're* for."

"I said a *real* doctor."

"Don't sell yourself short." She ruffles my hair and I want to rip her arm off. "Don't you want to see what I got?" she says.

"The sail?"

"Not *that*." She hands me a newspaper, something in English, and folds it to some page near the back. "Look."

I can't make out too many words, but it doesn't take much to know why she's excited. The photograph, after all, looks like another blurry rendition of the glimpses of the monster from La Manza's apartment.

El Diamante.

"Where did you find this?"

"That old bastard La Manza was at the market. Stole it out of his bag." She grins. "Look. This week. Off the coast of Algeria, how long do you think it would take?"

"From here? Three weeks, maybe."

"I thought maybe two . . ."

"Closer to four if anything."

"Damn. We better get moving, then."

"What? Now?"

She waves the newspaper at me. "It's there *now*. Who knows how long it stays in one place?"

Oscar moves a little bit in his sleep and pinches my sleeve with his fingers, mumbles something that sounds a lot like *Dad.*

"We don't even know how to kill it, Bela, and unless the method turns out to be two or three rounds from a handgun, we don't have it."

"We've got a blowtorch, plenty of rope . . ."

"Are we going to Algeria?" Zulu says. "Can I ride a camel?"

We both ignore her. "Beleza," I say. "Listen to yourself."

"Listen to *myself*?" She stands up. "This is our chance. You think we're just going to stumble on another clue about it again?"

"I don't want a clue!" I say. "I don't support this plan! Especially when we have nothing, no weapons, barely a boat—"

"Well, I didn't support getting robbed blind by a pirate."

"What the hell does that have to do with anything?"

"It means we don't trust your instincts."

"Oscar's *sick*." I hate using him like this but it's my last card to play.

"We're leaving at sunrise," she says.

COLD WATER

Salt gets everywhere when you're at sea. Under your nails, between your teeth. Your clothes are never dry, but your skin is always cracked from all the salt.

When was the last time I was *clean*? When was the last time my throat didn't hurt?

You fall asleep to the waves. You wake up to the waves.

Your hands are calloused, your feet are bleeding, your tiny boat is too big for the two of you to handle while Zulu naps and Oscar convalesces.

"We're not going to make it out of this one alive, are we?" I ask Beleza one night.

She's sitting by the wheel, staring out into the still water like she's waiting for something to rise up and eat us.

"Do you care?" she says, eventually.

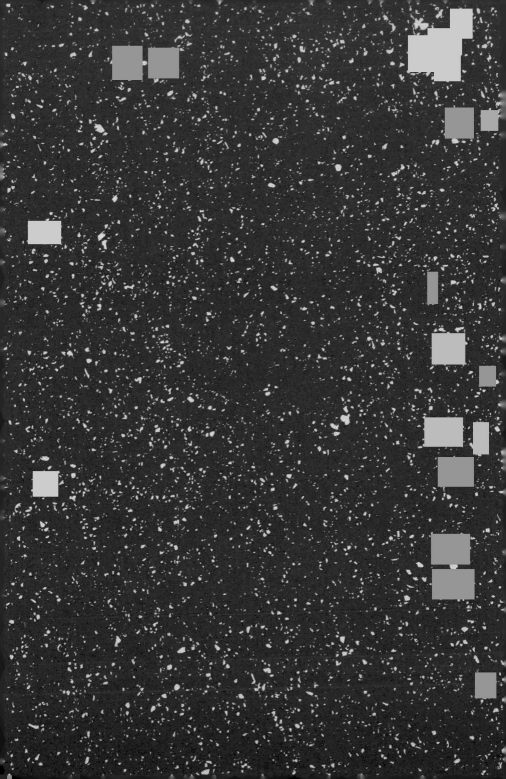

FROTH

We haven't been out at sea three days when I see it, that telltale perfect circle of foamy water out in the distance. Since we weren't able to replace our radar, watch duties are more important than ever. Oscar still can't stay awake for more than a few hours at a time. Beleza, on the other hand, rarely sleeps. But she does now, propped up in her captain's chair, and I'm watching alone when the froth crops up.

When we were little, we had to memorize all the different monster signs. Sudden thunderstorm might be nothing, sure, but it might be a toneda. That eerie, high-pitched howl that you'll never mistake for anything else once you've heard it? Sarkhayir. And a perfect circle of foamy water in the middle of a still sea?

That's a devorar.

"Beleza!"

She's up in a second, shaking sleep out of her hair and drawing the pistol. "What?"

I point.

"Shit," she whispers.

"I'll get the knives," I say. "When it gets close enough we'll just start throwing."

"No," she says.

"What other choice do we have?"

"Go to the mainsail," she says.

"Beleza?"

"We're steering away," she says.

"If we don't take it out, it's going to eat the next dozen ships that come along."

"That's their problem," she says. "We don't have the supplies to spare."

I'm already almost at the mainsail—I'm nothing if not good at taking orders—but I stop and just stare at her. My big sister. This girl I know better than I know anyone, whose bravery I used to wear like a blanket.

"We're going to let people die because we don't want to use up a few knives?" I say.

"Don't argue with me, Indi."

"What the hell is wrong with you?"

"I'm just being—"

"Then why the *fuck* are we doing this?" I yell. "We're not even saving people anymore. Why don't we just *stay on dry land*?"

"Indi, *change course!*" She's over by the wheel now.

And she looks terrified.

And I put it together.

"You're not trying to save supplies," I say. "You just know we can't beat that thing."

She won't look at me.

"You *know it*!" I say. "You know we can't take down a damn *devorar* and you're still leading us—"

"Change course," she says, staring out at the circle of foam.

I do. We don't speak for five days this time.

PERFECT CIRCLE

I don't really know how it happens. Maybe the devorar was following us. Maybe we've been making a giant circle in the middle of the ocean this past week instead of pointing toward Algeria and a monster we can't beat; maybe we're that bad at this. Or maybe we just have the shittiest luck of any four orphans I've ever run into.

But this time, when Oscar screams *Beleza!* in a voice that's still hoarse from coughing and coughing, the whirlpool is a few dozen meters away from swallowing us whole.

We have nothing. We can't do this. We have *nothing.*

So time stops.

Do I care? Do I *care*, Beleza?

Have you heard his voice? Have you seen her face? Heard their laughs that I can barely remember anymore, heard her crying for her mother, seen him squinting out to the horizon?

I could have been so much more.

I could have—

"Indi." Beleza forces a rope into my hands. "We have to trap it. We can't kill it long distance."

"I know." I take a deep breath. "Okay." I look at Oscar leaning over the rail, knife in hand, waiting. "Where's Zulu?" I whisper.

"Sleeping," Beleza says.

"Good. Good."

She draws the gun, clicks off the safety. "Get ready."

"Uh-huh."

The ship starts to shake and list to one side as the whirlpool creeps closer. *Come on come on come on.*

Maybe that's how my parents went—eaten by the sea instead of by a monster. It's not like I know how El Diamante works. I know nothing. We have nothing.

Oscar twirls the knife in his hand, waiting.

Devorars have poison blood—they're one of Beleza's favorites to siphon for her arrows that Hura probably now has stashed somewhere. Poison blood means poison blood flow. Blood flow means circulation.

"Strangle it," I whisper.

Beleza looks at me. "What?"

"Get the rope around it, tighten it, squeeze off—" I say, and then the monster roars. Cutting through the top of the deep rumble I can hear Zulu's scream. I can't worry about that right now. The monster's up.

It's a small one. Must be young. Intellectually, I know that. But when Beleza says, "God, it's huge," I know exactly what she means.

It's too big.

Oscar either doesn't know or doesn't care. He goes at it with our knives, the ones we use to butcher tentacles and slice bread—how the hell are we going to butcher tentacles and slice bread now—heaving them over the side of the ship and into the devorar. Its green skin shivers, the knives stuck out of it like antennas.

I get to Oscar just in time to move him out of the way when the monster rears up. Oscar's breathing hard, and I feel his shoulder blades shuddering under my hands. He threw those knives with everything he had in him, but he's so far from a hundred percent and it's *too big*—

"Get back!" I yell at him, and by some miracle he listens, and I spin a length of rope around my hands and get it solid in my palms before I sling it over. Beleza unwinds next to me as fast as she can, but the devorar is starting to spin. Trying to whip up another whirlpool. Trying to drag us under.

God, I hope it eats us quickly. Drowning takes so long.

"Stop it," Beleza says to me. "Stop thinking."

"Shut up and get me more rope!"

Oscar's caught his breath by now and he's behind me, tossing rope into the water. When the devorar rears its head up again—they can't breathe very long underwater—we're ready, and the two of us sling a length of rope around its neck and pull.

It screams.

Beleza throws our last knife into its eye. It keeps screaming.

Oscar and I tighten the rope, pulling, pulling. It stops bucking, its neck crackles, and its head slides sickeningly sideways. And off. Vertebrae fall around our ship like confetti and we stand there on the deck, out of breath, pale, alive, horrified.

"Can I come up?" Zulu calls from below.

Beleza wipes her hands on her pants. "Go get her," she says to me. "She's got poison blood to cook off."

Oscar staggers a little and sits flat on the deck.

"I don't want her to see this," I say.

"What?" Beleza says. "We won."

"We tortured it," I say. "It's . . . look at this. It's gruesome."

"We didn't exactly have the luxury of being humane, Indi."

"That's my point."

"So what, we keep her away from hunts until we have the supplies to make neat kills?"

"*Yes.*"

Beleza snorts and starts down the stairs, but not before mumbling, "Get over yourself, Indi."

And somehow that's just it.

Get over *myself*? At what point have I gotten to think about myself for one second? When has any of this ever been about what I want, and more than that, how is trying to keep my baby sister away from just one moment of carnage about what *I* want? What do I want? What do *I* want?

"Drop me off," I say.

She slows but doesn't stop, snorts again. "What?"

"Make port somewhere and drop me off. I'm done. And I'm taking them."

She stops now.

"You can come or not," I say. "I don't care."

"We're really doing this again?" she says, as if I threaten to walk off all the time.

"I have never done this before," I say, and I watch her face change as she realizes I'm right. That this is the first time I haven't just let it sit unspoken, haven't just mumbled it under my breath.

"What do you want me to say, Indi?"

"Nothing. This isn't a threat or a discussion. I'm not trying to fight with you. It's just a fact. I'm leaving and I'm getting them out of this sick revenge plot of yours before you get them killed."

"I'm not going anywhere," Oscar says.

I stare at him.

"Don't be stupid," he says. "I'm not going to be some lub."

I'm too late.

"It's not about that anymore," I say. "You don't see what she's leading you into?"

"She's my *sister*, you shitbag," he says to me. "I'm not going to abandon her."

"And I'm not going to let you *die*," I say. I hear little footsteps on the stairs, and Zulu climbs onto the deck.

"What's going on?" she says.

"We're going to go somewhere nice, okay?" I say. "Somewhere you can go to school."

"You don't have any money," Beleza says. "You think you're just going to step onto land and suddenly everything will be perfect? She doesn't have a birth certificate. How are you going to get her in school?"

"I'll figure it out!"

"How? You've never figured out anything on your own. You've never done *anything* on your own. And now you think you know better than me how to take care of these kids, you arrogant little shit?"

"Oh, you're taking care of the kids by doing this?"

"I'm making a safer world."

"And getting them killed in the process."

"I'm teaching them to honor their parents," she says. "What the hell are *you* doing?"

Zulu looks at me, and then Beleza. And then she walks past Oscar and goes to Beleza and raises her arms to be picked up. "What's going on?" Zulu says.

I feel seasick.

"Indi's going to take a vacation," Beleza says.

"Screw you."

"You have anywhere particular you want to go?" she asks me. "Or should we just let you off wherever you can feel the sand between your toes."

I'm suddenly extremely sure that I'm about to cry.

Shit.

I hold out my arms. "Give her to me."

"Don't think so," Beleza says.

"Dump me wherever," I say, and I go below deck alone.

A MATTER OF TIME

I never saw any of this happening, not really, not like this. But one thing that seems particularly unbelievable is that I don't talk to them in the nineteen or so hours between when I tell Beleza to drop me off and when she actually does. I've never done any kind of silent treatment with the kids.

Not that that's what this is, because I'm not mad at them, exactly.

I just don't have anything to say to them.

Because what is there to say? I hand-raised those kids like baby chicks, and they pick her? They pick this life? What do I say, *I thought you liked me best*? I'm not going to look at those little faces and count down when's the last time I'm going to see them again before I leave and they get swallowed up by the ocean or a monster a few days or weeks from now because Beleza was too stubborn or they were too stupid or

I didn't think of the perfect thing to say to convince them until it was too late.

I'm not going to do that. I'm not going to go on deck and watch them look at me with their sad, alive little eyes. Or maybe they're up there laughing at me throwing my temper tantrum or whatever they think this is.

I need to come up with some perfect thing to say? I've been their compass their whole lives, and now I need one perfect sentence to get them to listen to me?

What has she ever done?

Yeah, she held them on her lap and soothed them after they got scratched up by monsters, but that's because I had to be kneeling on the deck stitching them up, and whose fault was it that they got hurt anyway? Yeah, she was always coming up with plans, she always knew where we were going and the best way to get there and why Mom and Dad were mad this time, but that's because I was taking care of the mundane shit so the three of them could look at us and tell themselves they were keeping it all together.

Or, you know.

Maybe that's entirely bullshit, because Beleza has been with them every second I have, and she's the one Oscar listens to, and she's the one Zulu imitates, and I'm not the only one who noticed that I don't fit in. That wasn't in my head.

Maybe they won't die.

Maybe Beleza's going to tell them to forget all about me in a few hours.

They'd listen. They listen to her.

BELONGINGS

I'm trying to pack a bag, but I have no idea what belongs to me. And Beleza borrowed my favorite shirt a while ago and it's not as if I'm going to ask for it back. That feels like admitting defeat, somehow. As if this whole thing isn't already admitting defeat.

We should be on land in an hour.

Beleza watches me hunting around under the bed, looking for nothing. "Last chance to change your mind," she says.

"Could change my mind a lot of times between now and land, technically."

"I don't know. Knowing you, you need a lot of time to dither back and forth about it."

"Huh. Wonder why I'm leaving."

"So it *is* just a hissy fit, then? *My big sister is so mean.*"

I zip up my backpack. "Whatever helps you sleep at night."

"I haven't slept at night in years, you insensitive prick," she says carelessly over her shoulder, on her way back up the stairs.

I keep looking for things to pack.

/

We're docked. Who knows where. Beleza doesn't take the kids onshore for lunch or to stretch their legs. She doesn't let them off the dock at all.

They don't argue. I thought they'd at least want to spend a few hours with me. It's so exhausting, being this wrong this many times.

It's also fucking devastating.

Oscar won't even look at me. He helps haul the *Salgada* in, tying crappy knots since he knows they won't be staying.

Zulu's hopping from one foot to another, her fingers in her mouth. "Where are you going to go?" she says.

I wrap her up in a hug. "I'll figure something out." She smells like sweat and smoke. I won't beg her to come with me. I spent so long telling myself that I wanted to get on land for her, and now I'm leaving without her. It turns out *that's* who I am, which means the best thing I can do for her now is tell her I'm not mad at her and tell myself I'm not leaving her to die.

I swallow and swallow and swallow.

"You don't let her do anything crazy, okay?" I say, because clearly I'm half-assed about this *being fair to Zulu* thing. "Turn on the puppy-dog eyes if she gets too reckless."

"Yeah."

She hasn't asked me not to go. Maybe Bela told her not to. I hope that's it. The only other alternatives are that Zoo doesn't care or that our family raised a little girl who's already too hard and stubborn to tell the people she loves to stay with her.

I have to get off this goddamn ship or I never will. I let her go.

"Oscar?" I say.

"Yeah, bye."

"Oscar."

He disappears belowdecks.

"He'll get over it," Beleza says from behind me.

I don't turn around. "Yeah."

"You got everything you need?" she says. She's all business. "Money?"

"I took a little."

"Yeah." She puts her hand on my shoulder and turns me around and pulls me into a hug. It's all muscle, slaps on the back. It doesn't even feel like her. "Good luck out there."

"Yeah. You too."

"Well, off you go, then."

I climb off and walk away and don't look back. *Don't look back.*

I think that I'm going to cry, but right when I'm far enough away from them and I look around to see if I'm alone and realize I have no idea where I am, not even the country—I start laughing so hard I can barely breathe.

And then I find a street address, a pay phone with Arabic instructions—clue one—that takes, after much trial and error, one of my Libyan dinar coins—pretty solid clue two—and call the only number I know.

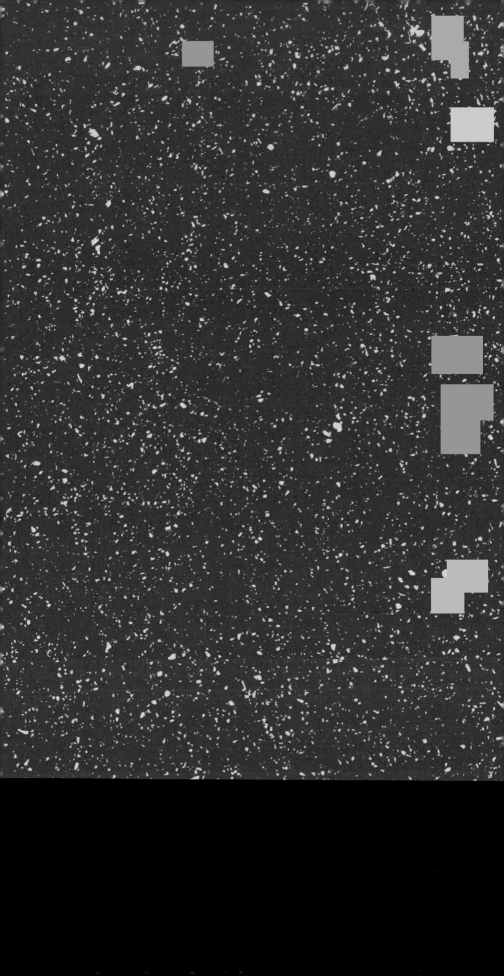

DEVIL YOU DON'T

Hura was, it turns out, in Tunisia, not far from Medenine, and it only takes her about four hours to appear at the hooka café where I'm nursing a coffee and still trying to figure out who and how I pay to get in on the hooka. She pulls up in a tiny yellow car, leans on the horn, and waves like we're best friends.

"I would have thought you'd still be hiding in the phone booth!" she says.

"Hey, we're finally somewhere I speak the language." I open the door to the backseat and toss in my duffel.

"You smell horrible," she says, as soon as I'm inside.

"Yep."

She starts driving. I don't know where we're going, but she reaches her hand out for the rest of my coffee and I give it to her because hey why not, she's taken everything else.

"So you're not going to beat the shit out of me?" she says eventually.

"You've probably got a bunch of goons who'd know to put out a hit on me if I did, right?"

She laughs without taking her eyes off the road. "Maybe you're smarter than I gave you credit for."

"So how'd you like the weapons?"

"I sold them!" Hura and her money. What a pirate.

"So did you think I was some crazy guy going around shooting imaginary monsters and that made me an easy target, or do you just rob everyone?"

"The second one," she says. "I believed you about the monsters. I told you, I've seen them before."

"Ah, and you're very trustworthy with your stories."

"I actually don't think I've ever lied to you. Directly."

"You told me once you were building a palace out of solid gold."

She raises an eyebrow. "So?"

I laugh, despite everything. Because of everything. "Hey, I guess if anyone could . . ."

"Yeah, you funded some gold bricks for us." She flicks on her turn signal, merges onto a major road.

"Where are we going, anyway?"

She shrugs. "Back where I came from."

"To the palace?"

"The palace right now is an apartment over a bar, but hey, it's not all that bad. They let me live there as long as I work."

That's a pirate's income for you. The first time I met her, she looked like she couldn't find two pennies to rub together, and then she got a crew and a fancy-as-hell ship, and now she's in a room over a bar. "You can stay with me," she says. "I don't care."

"I'm not sleeping with you," I say. "Anymore. I have some amount of pride. Maybe. Somewhere."

"That's fine. I'm with this guy Avraham right now."

It's weird; I would have thought I'd have some amount of jealousy in me. But being with her here is so much easier than it should be. Easy enough that it's draining all the tension right out of me, sexual or otherwise, like a squeaky-clean drain.

I am just happy to see her, in this ridiculously simple way. I was surprised when she answered and even more surprised when she agreed to come get me with next to no hesitation. So after a while of driving, I give up and ask why.

"I like you," she says.

I wait for her to say more, but I guess that's it.

And, God help me, she robbed us blind, but I like her too. I'm glad she's sleeping with Avraham.

It could have been worse. She could have robbed us at sea, left us stranded. She could have run off with our whole ship and not just our supplies. She could have hurt me, or kidnapped the kids, tried to hold them for ransom. She could have kept me captive on a ship my whole life fighting a war I couldn't win.

She's bad, but she's not the devil, in other words.

"So what's it like being on your own?" she says.

"Is that what you call this?"

"Sure," she says. "No little critters."

"I've been away from them for a few hours before, you know," I say, though I can't exactly remember when the last time was.

"So it's nice and familiar?" she says. "Sinking into a hot bath?"

"You just really want me to take a bath," I say.

"I really, really do."

/

And so I move in with Hura above the bar. We sleep in the same bed, most of the time, though every once in a while one of us exiles the other to a couch or a chair down in the bar after closing, so we can share a bed with someone for something besides sleeping, since all Hura and I do is conk out a few feet from each other without so much as a handshake. "We have a green-card marriage," Hura says to one of the regulars, explaining our relationship, and I don't know what that means exactly, but it somehow seems right nonetheless.

Hura drives a cab, that's where she's currently getting income. She says she hasn't been out to sea since Ukraine, and she doesn't show any signs of wanting to head back out. I start working at the bar, slowly at first, just drying glasses, but soon I can mix drinks with the best of them; Avraham even teaches me his secret garnish on ouzo. And listening to the problems of these normal people who speak a language I know is like, well, sinking into a hot bath.

The shock of it all is that I'm functional. Every time I wake up in the morning not shaking like sea legs, I can't believe it, for a while.

Of course I miss them. Of course I worry about them, and wonder if they're even alive. I guess I thought I would have heard from them, which is stupid, since it's not as if there's a way they could reach me. Knowing that, the weeks pass pretty easily. It doesn't mean they're dead. It doesn't even mean they're angry at me. They're off in their own world and I'm here in mine. They have each other, and I have . . . Hura, and I have my friends at the bar, so really I have no one, but I'm fine. I'm actually fine.

I talked such a big game, but I honestly didn't think I could do it. I thought I'd do a few days on land and fall asleep sobbing so hard that Beleza would hear me like a foghorn and sail right up and scoop me back where I belong.

But I just go about my days, doing nothing really, not saving any worlds, not fighting with any sisters, not stressing about any brothers, just washing dishes and sleeping next to a pretty girl and sweeping the floor and laughing with strangers, playing the part of someone who's listening.

The steady floor beneath my feet, the quiet nights, the dry clothes. Nobody thought I could do it, and I can.

I'm not sure I really belong anywhere, but this isn't so bad. Maybe 'isn't so bad' is 'happy'?

ZULU

About three weeks into my job here, a middle-aged guy comes into the bar late and asks for tea. There's hardly anyone else here, just me and Avraham behind the bar and a loud small group of regulars at their table in the corner. I'm not sure we have any means to make tea, but Avraham disappears under the counter and emerges with a blue china teacup and starts working away.

The guy drinks his tea and talks to Avraham for a while in a language I don't recognize. It's eerie; I've gotten so used to everyone speaking Arabic, which I understand as well as it's possible for me to understand anything other than the weird amalgam language I used to speak. Hura says my Arabic's gotten pretty good.

She comes in then, all draped in her bracelets and silk scarves like usual. "Hey," she says to me, ignoring both the customers and Avraham. I think they're in another fight.

They're always arguing about how to run the bar or spend their money or their evenings.

"Where have you been?" I ask while she shakes dust off herself.

"Had to see a guy about a boat," she says.

"Are we headed back out?" I say. It's out of my mouth before I even think of it, and I swear I feel myself blushing.

She, of course, doesn't let it go. "You gonna follow me wherever I go, puppy dog? You know you can do whatever you want, right?"

"I know that."

"I thought you hated the ocean."

"I never said that."

She slides up to the bar and hits it until I flip over a glass for her and fill it with whatever's nearby. "I just hate staying in one place," she says.

"I don't mind it." It almost feels true, the more I say it.

"Then don't come with me," she says, like I'm stupid.

I look at Avraham. Talk about no jealousy—he could not care any less about anything Hura and I do together. "Could I even stay here without her?"

Avraham shrugs. "Long as you're working, what do I care where you sleep."

"Huh."

"Who knows if he could even handle it," Hura says to Avraham, grinning. So maybe they're not fighting, or maybe she just won't let pass any opportunity to make fun of me. "All on his own. Maybe he'd fall apart like a baby bird."

"I'd be fine on my own," I say. "It's not like you're around here holding my hand as it is."

"Hmm," she says. "True." She drains her glass and sets it down. "Who would have thought. Little Indi knows how to take care of himself after all." I go over to the other side of the bar to wipe down counters and let her and Avraham make angry sexy eyes at each other.

They've retreated upstairs by the time our few customers have cleared out, so it looks like I'm sleeping in a booth tonight. I flip over the OPEN/CLOSED sign on the front door and bus the booth. Then I start cleaning up after the tea-drinker, and I pick up the teacup and realize there's a bite missing from it. There's a large chip in the rim and a very clear set of teeth marks that were absolutely not there when Avraham served him.

The guy took a bite out of the teacup.

Did he swallow it? Did he spit it out somewhere? I can't find it anywhere. I wonder if he chewed it up. I'm on my hands and knees by his barstool looking for any sign of the missing piece—I don't know *why*, it's not as if I'm going to reattach it; I guess I just think that if I find it, that will somehow give me an explanation—when it occurs to me how much I want to show this to Zulu.

Avraham and Hura won't think it's as funny as I do. Oscar and Beleza wouldn't have either. It's just Zulu who would appreciate the hell out of this, who would want to speculate on the guy's motives with me for hours, who would be on the floor with me looking for a bite of a teacup.

It's not worry, not obsession, not a gross knot in the pit of my stomach. Just this feeling that I've seen something and it would be funnier if she were here.

I shake it off. As best I can.

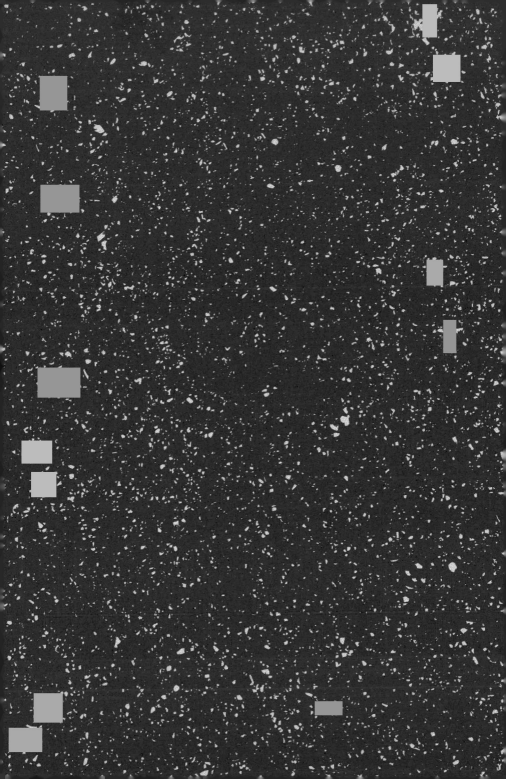

OSCAR

Hura's been warning me about the crime here since five minutes after we rolled into town, but it's not until about six weeks after I start working at the bar that we really have an issue. I stumble out of bed around noon to go open up, and the lock on the front door is cracked open and the cash register is empty. There wasn't a lot of cash left in there to begin with, and the broken lock isn't a lot of damage, but it's definitely enough to be disconcerting, and enough to piss off Avraham, whose whole point in stationing us over the bar was so we'd wake up for this kind of shit.

Hura leans against the doorframe with her arms crossed, watching me mess with the broken lock. "Do you know what you're doing?" she says.

"I do."

"Mm-hmm."

"I grew up at sea, remember?" I say. "You think we hired someone every time our ships broke down? We can't all assemble hordes of pirates at will."

"If the whole world could do the things I do, I wouldn't want to live in it."

"Yeah, me neither."

"You have a lot of locks on your boats, then?"

"I've actually always wanted to do stuff like this," I say. I dump the lock on my lap and straighten a broken hinge with Avraham's freakishly sharp pliers. "Maybe work on cars or something."

"I'm not letting you anywhere near my car."

"I don't know why you think I'm not good at anything." I hold up the hinge. "See?"

She just rolls her eyes. "Go build me an airplane."

The lock looks good and works well and we test it over and over, slamming ourselves against the door, demanding money from each other in stupid accents. Avraham is so impressed that he has me redo the locks on the windows, too, and then he smiles and says he might as well put that new coat of paint on the ceiling, now that he knows no one can come in and walk off with the bar. He laughs like he's hilarious while Hura rolls her eyes, but later I catch her giggling to herself about the bar disappearing in the middle of the night. It reminds me of Beleza and me, how we used to talk about me living in her pocket.

Except two nights later, we're broken into again, and this time the entire cash register is taken, like someone really did put it into their pocket.

"I don't get it," Hura says. "Are they going to sell the register on the black market? I don't think you can get that much for it."

"How'd they even do it?" Avraham said. "The thing was bolted down." He looks at Hura. "Aren't you supposed to be our criminal mastermind? You explain this."

"I don't do petty crime," she says. "Find a common thief and ask him."

"Pleased to say I don't know any damn common thieves," Avraham grumbles, and he gets to work sanding the place on the bar where the register was pried up.

"How about you?" Hura says to me. "Know any pickpockets?"

"Just one," I say. "But I don't know how to reach him anymore."

BELEZA

I don't get sick very often, maybe because despite our grubby lifestyle, we really only have each other for trading germs back and forth. I've had food poisoning a few times and some infected wounds and a very memorable bout of botulism, but getting sick like a normal person is pretty rare for me. So the cold I catch from a pretty, drippy-nosed girl at the bar takes me by surprise. I don't handle it that well.

Hura rolls her eyes and brings me tea in our bed above the bar. "You're pathetic."

I mostly blow my nose and glare at her.

I get the day off work to avoid infecting anyone else. There's not much to do up here—we don't have a TV or even a radio, since we mostly only come up to sleep—and I've already read the one Portugese book and five Arabic books on our rickety bookshelf ten times over. So I spend a few hours just lying still and looking out the window, watching a few people come in and out our front doors, watching most people walk right past us, watching Hura leave on a few grocery runs.

There's this thing that happens when you see someone you know amidst a lot of strangers. It's like they're lit from the inside, or like they're in color and everyone else is in black-and-white. It has nothing to do with whether you like them; I know this for a fact, since I'm very unsure on whether I like Hura. It's just the familiarity of it. I remember when Mom and Dad would come to get us after they'd been out on a trip, how they'd appear in the lobby of our hostel or shelter or we'd see them walking down the street and they'd just glow.

So I see that a few times today when Hura reappears. And I feel the same way I used to when I saw my parents. I never told anyone, for obvious reasons, but whenever I saw them after a long absence, I'd get so startled that I'd want to run away. The jolt when I saw them, how much they stood out, made me feel exposed and put off-guard. I should have been running to them and hugging them like Beleza always did, and instead I just wanted to go back to when everyone was dull and the same and nobody could scare me like that.

I felt a lot more guilty about this when it was my parents than I do now that it's Hura. I can't say it eats me up inside that I don't feel an urge to sprint down to the street when I see her walking by on the sidewalk.

But the gnawing shame about it regarding my parents, coupled with the boredom, makes me dig out their notebook. I don't think my siblings knew I took it. Beleza never looks at it anyway. She says she has the important parts all memorized.

I wonder if that includes the part about the treasure. I guess it doesn't really matter now.

Nothing matters now, really. I have this quiet nice life and a cold.

She's just so *angry*. Beleza. Going on this reckless revenge mission. And I'm fuming about that, just a little, when I turn a page in their notebook and it suddenly occurs to me: Beleza thinks our parents are alive.

She's not in this for revenge. She's looking for Mom and Dad.

I thought she was just faking it for the little kids.

I'm such an idiot. She actually thinks they're alive. That's why she won't talk about it. That's why she won't listen to me.

My sister.

Sometimes when I was younger she'd go off on hunts with them, and I'd stay back somewhere with the little kids. And Beleza would be the one who would come find us after, while our parents were taking care of affairs at the dock. And she'd stand out in the crowd brighter than a damn lighthouse.

And I never wanted to hide from her. I always ran to her.

Hura comes in late and slides into bed next to me. "Come here, you mess," she says, and I let her haul me into her. I rest my head on her shoulder.

"I'm glad I left them," I say.

"Good."

"But it's time to go back."

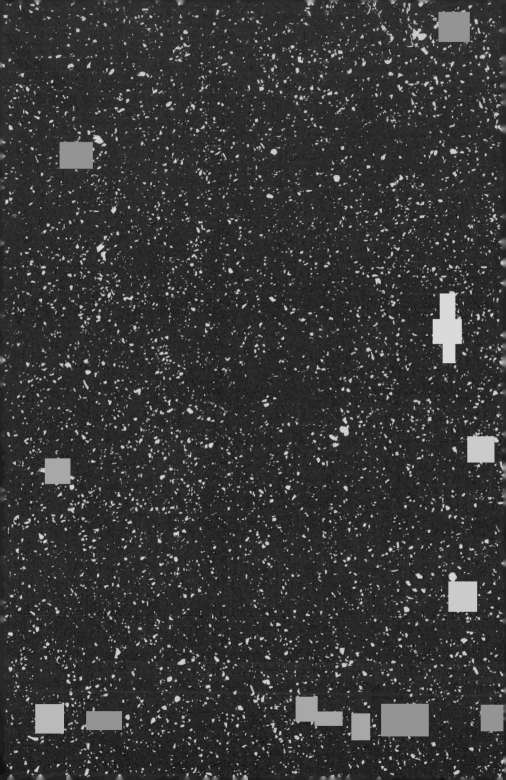

BOMBS AWAY

Hura says she's coming with me.

"I'm sick of Avraham," she says. "Clingy."

"What about the bar?"

"I think he can handle the three customers a day."

Before I can think of a good reason to leave her behind, she disappears into her pirate underworld for a night and comes up with news of weird weather patterns close to Madagascar. Cold rains, huge waves, even a ship gone missing a few days ago, rumors of weird noises from the water. It's an older lead than I would have liked, but it's a hell of a lot better than sailing around aimlessly like I was going to.

"So we just get close and radio?" she says, stuffing a few shirts into my duffel.

"Our radio's broken," I say. "We're going to have to actually find them."

"You guys have never heard of smartphones, huh."

"What?"

"Never mind." She closes the duffel. "We'll find them. If they're anything like you, they'll be pretty easy to track."

They're a lot like me.

Hura has a ship ready—nothing special, but it beats the *Salgada* by a mile—and it just needs a little caulking before we're ready to go. I get some canned food to unload below deck and discover a few rifles—*my* rifles—and half a dozen harpoon guns. *My* harpoon guns.

"Thought you sold it all," I say.

"I couldn't sell *all* of it," she says. "Not after hearing my odds of running into a damn monster every time I turn around."

I sit on the deck and check the sails for holes. "You know you're probably going to see one soon, right? In the flesh? A big one that's definitely going to kill us all."

"Nah, I've got good weapons." She winks. Pirate.

Setting out to sail feels, obviously, incredibly familiar, and there is a part of me that's comforted by that, but it takes all of five minutes at sea for me to be sure that I definitely haven't had any personality-changing revelations when it comes to sic life. I took a shower right before we left, an obnoxiously long one, and I'm already filthy again. Salt just sticks right to you.

"So did you always want to be a pirate?" I ask her, somewhere around Egypt.

She hums a little but doesn't answer, even when I push.

She's a great sailor, easily doing the work of me and a sibling single-handedly. I help her get through a small storm near Eritrea, but mostly she sends me down below deck to study up. "We don't know much about this thing," I keep telling her. "Rereading a few paragraphs over and over isn't going to help."

It's one of the nights I've fallen asleep with the notebook over my face that she shakes me awake, her voice lower and harsher than I've ever heard it. "I'm getting something on the radio," she says. "Come here."

I follow her around the corner from the bunks, where her radio's stashed. There's a voice coming through the handset, but the static's so heavy that I don't recognize it at first.

And then I do.

In stuttered French, then extremely broken Malagasy, and finally intelligible Arabic, my little brother: "Backup, please, is anyone close, please? Anyone? We need help." He fixed the radio. Such a scrappy kid.

"Coordinates, Oscar, come on," I whisper.

"One-three-point-two-eight by five-one-point-two-four," he says.

"That's my boy." We're close.

EL DIAMANTE

It's a deathly still sea, just this quiet sound in the wind, like a whisper, until it isn't.

It starts with a crack off in the distance, something like thunder, but from the depths of the ocean instead of from the sky. Hura reaches for my hand while I let the line slip through my fingers, unsure if I'm going to slow us down as quickly as possible or take our jibbing up a notch and get there faster.

And then I see, coming from the east, maybe eight hundred meters out from us, a little brown smudge of a rickety little sailboat.

And I recognize her right away. My *Salgada*. She shines like a bonfire.

"That's them," I say.

"Does that mean that's—"

And up it rises.

It's either closer than I thought or it's just so, so massive; I can't tell at first. Water pours out like a fountain, and our boat tosses, and I have no idea how our shitty *Salgada*'s going to survive the waves, let alone the monster that's spiked up, huge and inanimate like a cliff right in the middle of the sea.

"Holy crap," Hura whispers.

It's not moving. It's just sitting in the water, gray-black and glistening. I can't tell if it sees us because I can't tell where its eyes are. I can't even tell where its face is.

"Get the guns," I say, and a second after she goes below deck I change my mind and follow her.

"What are you doing?" she yells.

"Hang on." I go to the radio and, thank God, it's showing my ship. I ping them and ping them and finally there's an answer.

"A little busy right now," Bela says.

I laugh. I can't help it.

"*Indi?*"

"Due west."

I hear her bark muffled orders at the kids, then a minute later, shrieking.

"You ready for this?" she asks me.

"Not remotely."

"That's my boy," she says.

There's a deafening noise halfway between a crack and a growl, and the sea tilts on its axis and Hura and I go flying across the cabin and slam into the starboard side. We curse and shake ourselves off and run for the guns.

"There's an autocannon on the deck," Hura says.

"Go!"

We run back on the deck and Hura starts feeding ammunition into the cannon, and I load one of the machine guns and start doing whatever damage I can to this monster, but it doesn't seem to care. We're still far enough away that I don't know how many of my bullets are even hitting, but God, it's getting closer and closer by the second. We're ages past being able to control the ship—I've never felt water this rough in my life, and it's all I can do to clamber back to my feet after I'm knocked down again and again and again—so I don't even know if the monster's coming closer to us or we're getting closer to it.

It must be the second one, because the monster looks like it couldn't care less about us. All it wants is the *Salgada*.

They're going after the monster with everything they can. Zulu has the tasers, Beleza's shooting, and Oscar's just trying to keep the ship afloat, running from one side of the deck to the other, hoisting the boom, winding line. One of Beleza's bullets catches El Diamante between its diamond eyes, and it roars again and rips one of its tails out of the water to slam it down in protest, and it's huge and brown and glistening and crackles like thunder and makes a wave so massive, it looks like my siblings and their boat are soaring up—

No, they're not going up. We're going *down*.

The ocean was not this close a minute ago. I was not this soaked a minute ago.

I am not going to die in a monster fight because I *drowned*. That is not how this is going to go.

Hura's looking at me, panting, sweat and saltwater rolling down her face.

The *Salgada*'s only fifteen meters from us.

"Hook and a rope," I say. "Now. Go."

"How big?"

"Whatever will hold onto the boom!"

She crawls across the deck, trying to stay steady, trying not to tip into the damn sea. "What are you going to do?"

"Keep shooting, I guess."

"It doesn't care."

"You have any other ideas?"

"Go back in time!"

I don't have time to joke with her. We're probably about to die.

More importantly, I can hear Zulu crying.

Hura's back, throwing a hook up and looping it over the boom. "All aboard?" she says. I boost her up so she can grab onto the rope, pull her back, and push her with everything in me.

She swings out halfway between our two ships, like dangling little monster bait.

El Diamante is just *watching.*

"Harder!" Hura screams at me, and the next windup and push gets her close enough. She springs off the rope and lands on the *Salgada*'s deck, and for a second I let myself imagine the kind of small talk she's going to make with my big sister until I get there. *Hi. Thanks for all your supplies. Did you know Indi makes a mean mojito?*

And then the rope comes back and I realize there's no way I can work up enough momentum on my own to swing myself over.

The deck is halfway underwater now.

There's a blast of fire from over there—I guess they're trying makeshift flamethrowers now. God, why is the ship that's sinking the one with all the weapons? All they've got over there is whatever guns they've scrounged up in the last six weeks, some hairspray fireballs, and Beleza's arrows. Maybe they can do it on their own, maybe they'll win this and I'll go down and maybe there's something poetic in drowning in a monster fight, and—

A rope appears, with a hook on the top attaching it to the *Salgada*'s boom and a hook on the bottom for weight that just about scalps me as it swings by.

Oh. *They* could just make a swing and push it from over there. Obviously.

I don't get scalped, but I don't get ahold of it either. I hear Oscar curse as it probably gores his hands on the way back—*I'm sorry, I'm sorry*—but he pushes it back out to me, good boy, my good boy. . . .

I grab it above the hook, twist myself away from it so it can't gore me in the stomach, and hook my feet onto it to yank myself up. I call to them, they pull, and I'm flying.

I somehow land on top of all of them at once, in some bloody shredded heap.

We gasp ourselves to our feet just as Hura's ship sinks all the way below the water. It's just us now, just this awful little boat and a mountain of a monster who has us trapped all in one place.

It opens its mouth and roars, spit stretching between its teeth, a smell like gasoline rising out of its throat.

And Beleza, in a last-ditch attempt, rips off Mom's necklace, pulls back her bow, and fires it into the roof of its mouth.

And the motherfucker dies.

CIRCLE ME

I know I should be stitching everyone up, checking for broken bones, going through the atlases to figure out the quickest route to get us all to a damn hospital, but we're too tired and happy and . . . *finished.* We just lie on the *Salgada*'s deck, my siblings and Hura and I, in a bloody, useless pile, belly-laughing until it hurts, which doesn't take very long but feels good anyway.

Eventually Zulu gets up on wobbly legs to start butchering some El Diamante for dinner, and Hura helps Oscar up to show him some swordplay, and it's just me and Beleza here, lying on top of each other. "So," she says. "Couldn't make it on your own, huh?"

"I was, actually." I roll over onto my stomach and prop myself up onto my elbow so I can see her. I make sure to jab her in the ribs a little for good measure. "I was doing fine.

Had a job. Shared a bed with a pirate who was sleeping with someone else. Lub life."

Bela laughs. "So what happened?"

I don't really want to tell her. I'm scared that anything I say will make it impossible for me to ever leave again.

"I know what you're doing. And I get it." I swallow. "You're my best friend."

She groans and grabs me by the ear, tucks me under her arm. "Sap."

I close my eyes. "Mmm-hmm."

At some point I fall asleep, lying right there, and I guess everyone else must have too, because when I wake up, Beleza's still underneath me, Oscar and Zulu are collapsed on top of each other a few feet away, and Hura's gone, along with all the weapons, all our money, all our monster meat, and our liferaft, our sail.

Don't ever trust a pirate.

END

We're too hungry to panic. Too tired. We lie on the bunk beds, letting the wind take us wherever the hell it wants with the makeshift sail we made from knotting together our bedsheets. We lie on top of each other, every once in a while one of us finding the energy to talk over the strange whispering sounds from the ocean. *Remember the time we, remember, remember . . .*

We don't cry. We just float.

"You can eat me," Beleza says. "If I die first."

"That's disgusting," I say. "We don't have a stove. I'm not eating you raw."

She laughs and holds her stomach.

"I want to die in the water," Oscar says. "I'd rather drown than starve."

"They say drowning's a shitty way to go," Beleza says.

"So's starving," I say.

"We're going to die of dehydration long before starvation," Oscar says.

"We can filter water forever," I say.

"No," he says. "Because we'll get so hungry and stupid that we'll forget how, and then we'll die of dehydration."

"Sure," I say.

Bela closes her eyes. "Is there anything that's just like falling asleep? I just want to fall asleep."

"I don't think so."

"I wonder what it was like for them," she says quietly. Mom and Dad.

"Quick," I say.

"I think so too," she says, softly.

We're quiet for a minute, then Oscar says, "Quick is overrated. I like it slow and tedious."

"Mmm," I say. "Then you're in luck."

/

The other three are on the deck, trying to fish with nothing for poles and nothing for bait, and I'm lying on my stomach on the bed flipping through the journal, just feeling the texture of the pages more than anything, when I realize something. I drag myself up on board. I feel like I weigh more than the ship does.

"Bela?" I say.

She looks at me. She has circles under her eyes so dark she looks like someone punched her.

"Do you have any idea where we are?" I say.

She looks around at the open sea like she's expecting to see a signpost. "I don't know. Vaguely. Why?"

I show her the notebook. "You hear that noise, right? Like whispering."

"Yeah." She snatches the book out of my hand, of course. "What is this?"

"It's the treasure."

She stares at it for a moment. "You know there's probably nothing there."

"Yeah, but don't you want your dying words to be *I told you so*?"

"Of course."

"Think we can make it there?"

She looks up at our bedraggled fake sail. "What have we got to lose? Zulu, get ready to turn. We gotta head toward Portugal."

AFTER THE MAP

"Mom and Dad would never take us out this way," Beleza says. "Too close to where we're from. Too many memories."

We've just been crashed around the deck, but now we have to keep a tight hold on the line because wherever we are, this weird alcove near Portugal that isn't detailed in any of our maps, is packed full of tiny islands. Barely big enough for the four of us to stand on, most of them, but plenty big enough to sink a ship.

"Do you ever miss it?" I say. "Before?"

She doesn't say anything for a while, and when she does it's just to gripe that none of these islands have any coconut trees on them.

"You know I forget your real name all the time," I say.

"You barely even have a real name."

"True."

"So what was it like out there," she says. She's not looking at me.

"It was like . . . trying to breathe underwater. Except it turned out I could do it. Maybe I'm part monster." I watch her quirk a little bit of a smile.

"Doubtful," she says.

"I came back because of you, you know," I say. "Not because I felt obligated to take care of them. Because of you."

She swallows, coughs out a laugh. "You feel obligated to take care of me, that's it?"

"Well, yeah, look at you—all we're doing is sailing and you're crying."

"I'm starving to death, asshole."

"Yeah, yeah, who isn't."

She frowns at something ahead and runs up to the wheel. "What the hell is that?"

"Where?"

"By that island, look."

"Huh. Shipwreck?"

"Maybe there are supplies!"

The last thing we want to do is get too close and run into some jutting-out bit of this dead ship, since literally the last thing we have on Earth is a ship that isn't sunk, so we stop and drop anchor a safe distance away. I knew the ocean would be shallow here with all these islands, but it's even more shallow than I expected. The anchor only drops about fifteen meters.

Beleza sheds her jacket and climbs up on the railing, preparing to dive in.

"I can do it," I say.

"You're shivering already," she says. "Stay."

It's a nice gesture, but she's in the water for all of a minute and a half before she's yelling, "Indi, come here!" So much for her good deed. God, I can't believe I have to swim right now. I'm so dizzy. Everything inside me just feels like sand.

I throw down the ladder so we can climb back aboard, and dive in.

Beleza's treading water near the wrecked ship. She looks pale, even for someone starving.

"Do you see anything?" she says.

I shake my head. "Without a mask, there's no way to look through all this." I don't know how we thought we'd get food, unless we assumed whoever was on this ship hoisted unsinkable cans of food over the mast like a flag as they were going down.

"It's Mom and Dad," she says.

"What?"

"Look."

God. She's right. This is our ship. It's torn apart and it's been rotting in the sea for months, but I know this ship like I know my family.

My family.

"Do you see . . . do you see bodies or something?" she says.

"Without a mask . . ."

"Right, right."

So we just keep treading water, over the wreckage of our family, over this crushed ship, probably over our parents' bodies.

"They weren't going after El Diamante, were they," Beleza says. "They were checking on the treasure."

"Yeah."

"And they just . . ."

"Something must have gotten them," I say.

"Or they weren't looking and steered into this island and just . . ."

"Come back to the ship," I say.

We swim to the *Salgada* without looking behind us and clamber onboard, dry ourselves off as best we can.

"Don't tell the kids," Beleza says.

"Okay."

"Let them think they went out like heroes."

I watch her put her boots back on and tie up her hair. Watch her shake herself off.

"Come on," she says. "Let's find them some treasure."

"Okay," I say. I think about heroes, and I hug my big sister so tight.

LAND

We wake up Oscar and Zulu when we get closer. Whatever it is, we should see it together. And we have nothing we need to rest up for now, anyway. They're cold and half asleep, and Oscar lets Zulu tuck under his arm while they sit on the deck, leaning against the mast, swaying with the waves breaking against the tiny islands.

"It's that one," she says, pointing out into the distance, showing me her compass. "See? It's gotta be."

I snag her wrist to take her pulse. "Okay."

"I'm fine."

"Is that smoke?"

"What?"

"Look."

My first stupid, starved thought is *Our treasure is on fire*, but luckily Beleza speaks before I can share it. "There are people there," she says.

"Oh thank God," I whisper.

"Thank God? They probably stole our treasure!"

"They probably have *food*," I say.

"Oh. Thank God."

"Or we can eat them," Oscar adds.

"If it comes to it," Beleza says simply.

We're not going to die.

I don't think I realized until this very second how much I didn't want to.

I take Beleza's pulse again, just . . . I don't know. To be sure. She lets me this time.

Oscar stands up as we get closer to the island. We can see tiny houses, cracked roads with a few sputtery-looking cars, kids playing in grass that seems too impossibly green to be growing out of sand. It doesn't look at all like my place in Tunisia. Here there are huge expanses between the houses, and all the buildings have low roofs with trees stretching up beside them. It's like something from another time. From a story.

"What is this place?" Oscar whispers. I'm not sure I've ever heard him whisper before. He sounds so much like our dad for a second.

Zulu tugs on my arm. "Did Mom and Dad give us an island?"

"No," I say. "There are people living here, see? It's their island."

"I knew it was gonna be people," Zulu says. Now that we're not going to die, I need to get her some more books.

Maybe there's a bookstore here.

Maybe there's a school here.

By the time we're close enough to the shore to drop anchor, there's a small handful of people standing on the shoreline. A girl a little older than Zulu, a girl who's maybe around Beleza's age, and two men who might be fifty or sixty. Besides the little girl, who looks excited, they look so suspicious, I wonder if we've just exchanged death at sea for death by trespassing.

Beleza throws down the ladder and climbs down with all the confidence of someone who isn't lost and who hasn't gone five days without food. She sticks out a hand to shake, and one of the older men takes it, but his eyes are still narrowed.

The older girl taps his shoulder and points to Beleza. I can't tell what they're saying from up on the ship, or even what language they're saying it in, but I see Beleza reach for her necklace—before remembering where it is.

I climb down.

"What's your name?" the man says. Portuguese. Of course.

"Indi," I say, but he's looking at Bela. It's funny. I used to be so weird about talking to strangers, there'd have been no way I would have jumped in to answer a question before Beleza. Now I don't even care if they're talking to me, apparently.

"Dalia?" he says.

Oscar snorts as he drops to the ground next to me. "Nobody calls her that." I nudge him.

Beleza doesn't look at us. She just nods.

And the guy breaks into this enormous smile. The littlest girl jumps up and down.

"You look just like your mother," he says.

And then he gives us each an apple.

HOME

The men are brothers, Davi and Heriberto, and they fill us in as they lead us to a rock by the road, while we dodge hordes of kids with soccer balls, moms with babies on their backs and arms full of shopping bags, dogs with sticks gripped between their teeth.

To them, our parents were heroes. They saved the island from, of all things, a morde d'eau. It had terrorized the island years and years ago, and our parents were the first people they'd call whenever something monster-related went wrong in the nearby sea. It usually wasn't monster-related, they say, but Mom and Dad always either checked it out or found someone who could.

I'm glad my parents were there like that for someone. But I wish it was us, and I probably always will.

"So what," Oscar mumbles to me, his mouth full of apple. "Is he taking us to the bank or something? Pay off their debt?"

No. He's bringing us to the tiniest house I've ever seen, at the end of a tiny dirt road off one of the bigger streets. There are other houses crowded around on one side, but just a wide expanse of grass on the other, like we've found the very end of the world.

"They built this a long time ago," Heriberto says. "We kept it nice for them because they said you'd need it someday."

He opens the door—I guess we'll need to get a lock—and leads us inside. It's just one floor, barely tall enough for me to stand up all the way, but it's filled with light and threadbare furniture and so many pictures of us.

Zulu, working on pure adrenaline, sprints to the fridge, but there's nothing in it.

Davi laughs. "Here, we'll find you something to eat. Why don't the rest of you settle in and we'll bring something over?"

"I'm going with the food," Oscar says, following right behind Zulu as she heads out the door without hesitation.

"I . . . ," I say, because I shouldn't let them go off with someone I don't know, because this is all happening so fast, because I don't even *understand*, but . . . I'm so tired.

I fall asleep on the couch without finishing my apple. The last thing I hear is my hair ruffling a little under Beleza's—Dalia's—hand, and her quiet voice: "You win, Indi."

/

When I wake up, the house is empty and the ground is so still. The kitchen table is heaping with food, and I'm too hungry to even care about where my siblings are. I sit down and eat everything I can get my hands on, whether it's supposed to be eaten with hands or not. I don't even recognize half of what I'm putting in my mouth and I don't care. Nothing has ever tasted this good.

I stand up. I feel like a new person, like I'm as strong as four of me.

I go outside. The sun is beating down. At the end of the dirt path up by the road there's a car broken down, and a few people are crowded around it. They have a tool kit but they don't look like they know what they're doing.

I jog over. "What's the problem?"

"Engine's too hot," a guy says.

"I can fix that."

"Yeah?"

"Yeah, I can fix it."

I'm almost finished when a soccer ball hits me in the back of the head and Zulu yells, "Sorry!" and Oscar laughs and laughs. Some kid retrieves it and kicks it to his friend, who kicks it back to Oscar and they go back to their game.

I stand up and wipe my hands on my jeans. "Where's Beleza?"

"By the ship!" Oscar shouts as he runs after the ball.

Of course she is. I wind my way down the streets and back toward the shore. There she is, loading on some food and a few guns.

I knew it. I knew it wouldn't last.

"We're not going," I say.

I don't know where that came from. But God, it felt good.

"We earned this," I say. "You earned this."

She turns around and gives me half a smile. "Apparently there's something terrorizing ships a few islands over," she says. "Want to go check it out?"

"You're crazy, you know that?"

"We'll be back before dark."

I cross my arms.

"Come on," she says. "I promise. Gotta be up early tomorrow, right? I told Zulu we'd get her ready for school."

I close my eyes and feel so, so warm.

"Okay," I say. "Just this once."

She grins.